SILENT SCREAMING

JESSE PULLINS

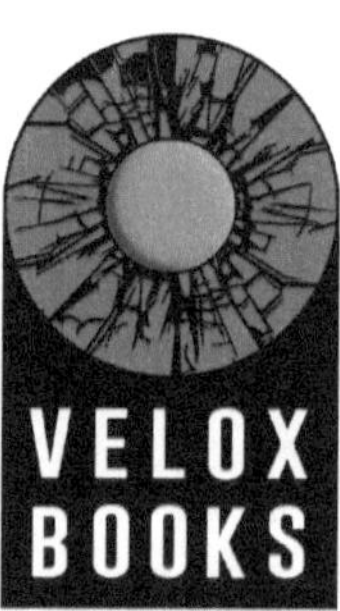

VELOX
BOOKS

**FOLLOW VELOX TO KEEP
THE NIGHTMARES COMING:**

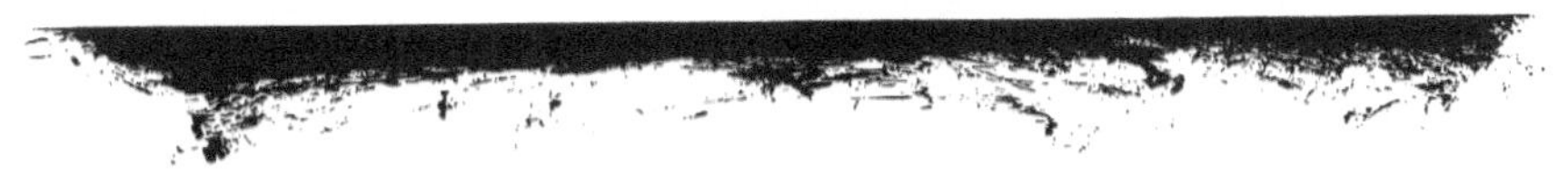

For my Mom. Here are more things to lurk past the tree line.

CONTENTS

COTTON THE CLOWN

I woke to the sound of a bicycle horn, a *ha-honk ha-honk* that seemed to echo around me. I blinked and lifted my head from the table, my head spinning and filled with fog. I tried to recollect where I was and how I got here, the pieces in my mind struggling to come together. I was trick-or-treating with my friends. We were only about an hour in, and then... nothing.

I tried to move and found that I couldn't. Each attempt was met with the sound of twisting rubber. I fought against it; the weight would stretch but ultimately keep me in place. I looked around the darkness of the room, my head swimming with confusion.

In front of me I heard a rip, followed by a squelching sound, like water hitting the floor. I tried to see it, but could only make out a little movement ahead. It sounded like someone was *eating*.

"Hello?" I called out hesitantly, wincing against the dark.

The squishing stopped, and I heard the heavy scuff of shoes across the floor. A light flicked on, and the brightness filled the room.

I was in what looked like a basement, and I was seated at a wooden table. Across from me was a teenager dressed as a pirate. I recognized them immediately; it was my friend Cody. That was it, I was out trick-or-treating with Cody and Amber, and we were walking down that cul-de-sac. The house at the end of the road had its lights off... and—

I gasped. Cody's mouth was duct-taped, and there was a trickle of blood drying from a nasty bruise on the side of his head. He was slumped over, unconscious in his own chair. I moved to help him, and forgot that my arms were stuck. I looked down to see they were tied to the chair, a comical yet terrifying coil of inflated balloon wrapped around each wrist.

"Aren't you a little old to be trick-or-treating?" a groan of a voice said from the corner of the room.

I looked to see a clown standing there, one hand on the light switch, the other covering his mouth. His hair was a poofy afro of blue and green, his make-up immaculate and shiny. His costume, however, was stained red. He let his hand slowly fall from the light switch, while keeping the other over his mouth. His eyes stared viciously.

"I'm sorry, whatever it was we did, I'm sorry—" I pleaded, racking my brain for the cause of all this. Slowly the details came back, the three of us going door-to-door, skipping our way to the last house at the end of the street. The lights were off, nobody was home.

"I asked you a question," the clown said, moving closer. His hand was still covering his lips. Why was he covering them? It didn't feel right.

"Y-yes," I answered. I had just turned seventeen, and Cody and Amber were a year older.

"*Good.* Honesty, I like that. Your friend wasn't so honest. Now look at her," the clown pointed to the head of the table.

A life-sized doll was seated there, a human replica of canvas and stitches. It looked like a girl with yarn hair and a ponytail, googly eyes in place of real ones, messy lipstick smudged on. A crude stitching ran around the doll's neck, barely keeping the head from falling off. A stethoscope hung lazily on her shoulder, where

I could see she was wearing a cheap nurse's costume. Amber had been a nurse.

"Please, just let me go!" I said, straining against the balloon restraints. They stretched, but they would not break.

The clown started to talk again, all the while keeping his hand up.

"I'll make you a deal. I'll ask a simple question, a fun question, and if you get it right, I'll let you go. Just some *clownin' around* for the road. What do you say?" he asked, gesturing to my costume.

I looked down at the polka-dots and fluffy cuffs I was garbed in. The memories flooded back, the three of us skipping. Cody, a pirate. Amber, a nurse. I was a clown. We saw the house at the end of the street, the house with its lights off. It was Cody's idea. We didn't think anyone lived there. We hopped the fence to the backyard, keeping quiet as we approached the back door. It was Cody's idea to break in.

"Help! Somebody HELP ME!" I yelled, my voice dry and scratched.

"Come on, now, I just wanna have some fun—" the clown said.

"HELP! HELP!" I continued.

"Just answer the question. *Or. I'll. Eat. Your. Insides!*" the clown screamed from behind his hand, the veins in his eyes popping. His voice was much louder than mine, like he had swallowed a microphone.

I stopped shouting and started to cry.

"There, that's much better," the clown said, and waltzed over beside Cody. He stood next to him and crouched down so he was level with me. His hand never fell. "My name is Cotton the Clown. What is my favorite... holiday... treat?" He said, staring.

Beside him, Cody started to stir awake. It was then I saw the squiggly line drawn around his neck, like a child's doodle in marker.

I thought of us breaking in through the back door with a rock and letting ourselves in. I wanted to go, but Cody and Amber insisted. The house looked abandoned, aside from the dust-covered dolls lining the walls. Each with googly eyes and stitched necks. I wanted to go, but we heard the scream. It sounded like it came from the basement.

"Well? What's my favorite holiday treat? *Answer me.*" The clown stared blankly from behind his hand.

I started to mumble. Cody opened his eyes and started to panic, muffled screams from behind the duct tape.

"What's that? I can't hear youuuuuuuuu." Cotton's eyes started to bleed and he winked, a *ha-honk* of a horn making me flinch.

"Cotton... candy?" I said, and the clown slammed his fists on the table. He uncovered his mouth and bared his teeth, teeth that were replaced by dozens of skittering fingers.

"THAT'S RIGHT. COTTON. CANDY," the clown screamed, and without warning, grabbed Cody by the head and shoulder. With a horrifying rip, Cody's neck split open as he screamed. A burst of fluffy pink exploded from his neck, sugary strands that the clown immediately started to feast upon. I screamed as Cody's eyes rolled back, and the clown stared at me as each sentient finger grabbed at the cotton candy.

———————

I woke up in the middle of the street, alone. It was dark out; the moon shining high above as I picked myself up. I looked around, each house long closed from trick-or-treating. Cody and Amber were nowhere to be found.

I heard a scream in the distance, and turned to look behind me. I was at the end of the cul-de-sac, in front of the abandoned house. The lights were off in every room in the house... all except the little one for the basement.

Standing in the window were two dolls, one dressed as a pirate, the other a nurse. They both reached for me, and the light went out.

BENEATH THE POWERLINE

Every day I drive to the local gas station and smoke cigarettes on my lunch break. I work in assembly on a clean campus, and there's no smoking on the premises. Luckily the gas station isn't far, and I get to have about twenty minutes of peace and quiet and decompress.

I do the same thing every time, meticulously watching the clock on the dash while my lunch break ticks away. There's a line of parallel parking styled spots on the side of the building and I pull up there, enjoying my first smoke while I watch the corn sway in the wind while the radio plays softly.

The gas station is less than a mile away, but my job is located outside of town in the country, so the space between places is filled with nothing but a cornfield, trees, and a stretch of power lines running high above. It's a very peaceful rustic getaway, and oftentimes I zone out, staring off into space, watching the corn sway as my eyes wander aimlessly.

Three days ago, I saw something staring back at me.

I don't know how long it had been standing there before I noticed it. At first, I acknowledged it like one would notice a tree they hadn't seen before. Suddenly becoming aware of an existence that didn't matter; except this tree was humanoid in shape, and by the looks of it, didn't have any skin. It was a few hundred feet away, but there was no denying the fact that something was terribly wrong with it.

An icy chill immediately ran up my back, triggering all of my nerves while I shifted uncomfortably in my seat. I looked around to see if anyone else had noticed it, but everyone was just going about their business, pumping gas or hurriedly leaving their car to head inside. I rubbed my eyes and looked again, swearing it had just been a trick of the light.

Not only was it still there, it had moved closer. It had drifted out of the corn slightly, leaning against the leg of the tall power line it was under. I could see the slight deviation of movement while it stood there, like it was breathing heavily and stopping to catch its breath. Even from so far away, I could see the specks of white for eyes staring at me, and an overwhelming feeling of foreboding tunneled towards me. It felt like I was going to get hit by a car, or a plane would crash on top of me. It's hard to explain.

It just... stood there. Staring at me.

As the seconds melted into minutes, I snubbed out my smoke and did what every other rational person would do. I grabbed my phone and tried to take a picture of it. It stood there while I opened the app for my camera, holding the same stare as I tried to get the camera to focus. It finally did, and I slowly zoomed in to try and get a decent view of it. But just as my thumb tapped the button to capture it... it disappeared.

Not like I looked away and then it was gone. It just vanished into thin air. Like it ceased to exist.

I sat there for a time afterwards, unable to shake the feeling that something was very wrong. The longer I sat, the more I wondered if I had just imagined it. Maybe the days of lack of sleep, fatigue, and stress were piling up and I was starting to daydream. Maybe I had dozed off and didn't notice? The days had felt so much shorter since daylight savings time. Maybe it was just a case of the seasonals picking away at my brain. I kept thinking of scenarios to justify such a thing, even as I pulled out of my parking spot and headed back to work.

I kept looking back to the empty spot in the corn under the power line expecting to see it again, but I saw nothing.

After I punched back in, I asked some people on the same line as me, ones that I knew would also go and smoke during the allotted time on lunch. I wasn't the only regular there, but I was the only person that saw it. Most told me I needed to get some sleep and stop staying up so late. Others suggested maybe it was just a *deer*, or maybe someone who lived out in the boonies trying to make themselves viral by scaring people in the corn.

In the end I laughed it off, but throughout the day I was unable to shake the feeling, stricken from what I saw. The dread continued to stay with me, even after I punched out for the day and headed home. It persisted through the night, and it made me paranoid when I hung out at home, and even as I crawled into bed.

I tossed and turned for a while, thinking of the red humanoid shape lingering in the distance. I kept waking up and looking at the doorway, expecting to see it. Each time, nothing. But the feeling of unease persisted, even as I felt myself succumbing to sleep.

That night, I dreamt of walking through the cornfield.

Chilly wind tossing my hair and whipping at my clothes. The corn swayed in the gust, a steady dance that moved across the crops as far as I could see. It was peaceful but engulfing, an intimidating embrace that made me feel small in the vast expanse of it. Dried husks crackled under my feet, and the mud tried to steal my shoes. I don't know where I am, and I start to feel the swaying stalks close in on me.

Above, the power line reaches towards the sky, looming over me like a sinister lighthouse. I look away from the swirling gray overcast, following the legs of the power line. I squint through the stalks to see, and I see a dark crevice in the ground ahead.

Beneath the power line there's a cellar door hanging open.

Beckoning me.

I wake to the sound of my alarm, drenched in sweat. A fog swirls in my head, oddly hungover from a sober sleep. I look at the doorway of my bedroom and find it empty. The sense of dread continues to loom.

I get ready for work and head in, thoughts of corn and the cellar door racing through my mind. I can't shake the thought of it, and it proceeds to pester me through the beginning of my shift. I try to busy my mind and focus on work, tightening fasteners on the brackets of air-compressors and running rubber hoses as the clock ticks away. Even as my hands work monotonously, I feel the weight of eyes on me. I constantly look over my shoulder, but there's never anyone there.

On my lunch break, I decided to return to the gas station. I convinced myself that I'm just being crazy, and there's no reason *not* to go and enjoy my daily smokes on my break. Just of the thought of them sounds so nice.

I pull into my usual spot and light up, feeling the weight ease off my shoulders after the first drag. I sink into my seat, keeping my eyes closed as I ignore the cornfield next to me, telling myself over and over: *there is nothing there.*

I gather the courage to open them, and I look at the cornfield.

The power line stands defiantly in the corn, and I feel myself sweating as I trace the length of the spire to the ground.

Beneath the tall structure, there is nothing.

I breathe a sigh of relief and laugh at myself, nearly coughing as I wipe the sweat from my brow. There is no skinned man. Only corn swaying in the wind.

I feel better having conquered the fear. I turn my music on, and a familiar song crackles over heavy static. I try to tune the dial, but the distortion only grows the more I tamper with it. In the end I turn the volume all the way down and decide I'm gonna run into the gas station and buy an energy drink. I suddenly feel parched, and the feeling of ice-cold electric carbonation sounds too good to pass up.

I shut off my car, get out of the car, and stop.

The skinned man is standing near the gas pumps, peeking out at me. His eyes are bright white and beady, his stare freezing me to my core. His limbs twitch, and he takes a step out from behind the pump, a bloody trail smearing the pavement with his footstep.

I break out of my fear and look around to see if anyone else sees him. But nobody does. It's like he's not even there. Even as he takes another step towards me, a woman in a hatchback pulls past him, nearly grazing him.

His skin is completely gone. Steam radiates from exposed bloody muscle, steady drips of red trickling down his arms and legs. He appears genderless, but his build is masculine. As the woman next to him gets out of the car and starts fueling, his mouth slowly hangs open, and he starts to scream.

A scream that nobody can hear but me.

I get into my car and I leave, tires squealing as I turn around in the lot. I keep watching him, terrified he's going to suddenly give chase and rip me out of the car. But he only reaches for me slowly, like he can barely move.

When I haul ass down the road, I watch for him in the rear-view mirror. He lowers his hand and vanishes.

Nobody believed me when I got back to work. I talked about the man with no skin, and his scream that no one could hear. The reactions were less entertained than the day before. Those who didn't laugh excused themselves awkwardly. Those that did neither just looked at me like I was crazy.

My shift crawled for the rest of the day. I was incredibly anxious, a cold sweat dampening my forehead as I looked around cautiously. Everywhere I looked I *swore* I saw the skinned man, but only to see an empty aisle or a part rack instead. People tiptoed around me or avoided me entirely, not wanting to draw attention to my increasing paranoia. I kept hearing his scream, the dry cry of an out-of-tune orchestra. Just thinking of it and seeing his open mouth made my skin crawl.

Once my shift concluded, I punched out and left work without a word. On the way home I kept looking around, still unable to shake the feeling of someone watching. I kept feeling someone staring at me from the back seat, breathing on my neck. Each time I would turn to look, there would be nothing.

Once home, I stayed inside for the rest of the day. I locked the doors and preoccupied my mind with watching TV, hopping restlessly from one streaming service to the next in search of something to draw my attention. I would occasionally peek out of the windows of my apartment to make sure he wasn't there but would only see the occasional passing car. Everywhere I looked, I saw those damned eyes staring at me.

That night I fell asleep on the couch, the muffled drone of an anime playing from the television. I don't remember when I dozed off, but I soon found my tired paranoia easing into a restless slumber.

In my dream, I returned to the corn. I was looking at the power line, watching it tower above me. At my feet was the open cellar, an echoing wind whispering from the dark opening in the muddy earth. Above, the sky swirls gray, and I look down just to see myself jumping in. I fall for a long time, plummeting through darkness silently.

There seems to be no end.

In the darkness below I see a faint red glow, a glimmer of light approaching me. I reach for it, hoping it will stop whatever is transpiring. As the light drifts closer, the darkness explodes with sound. The sound of an out-out-tune orchestra.

I wake up covering my ears, the sounds brutal and deafening now that I'm awake. My apartment shakes under it, and I look around to find the source, only to end up screaming.

The skinned man is on my balcony, his mouth opened wide in his silent tortured scream. He places his hands on the glass of the slider, leaning in to see me. The feeling of primal fear swallows me, and I fight the urge to cry. Vomit churns in the confines of my stomach.

As suddenly as my dream ended, the skinned man vanished, once again leaving an empty space in his wake. I spent the rest of the night cowering in my room, hiding under the blankets and flinching at every sound. I slept restlessly, plagued by thoughts of being burned alive, my screams echoing over the field of corn.

Today, I woke up to my alarms, flinching over the thought of the out-of-tune orchestra. I crawled out of bed slowly, my limbs aching from my restless sleep. The thought of getting ready for work fled my mind, and I thought only of the power line in the cornfield. I looked outside, and saw the sky was unusually gloomy. My skin crawled with goosebumps that refused to leave, and my hair stood on end. Even in my groggy state, the feeling of being watched refused to leave.

I looked everywhere for the skinned man, begging this to stop.

It has to stop. I can't keep doing this.

Today I got dressed and headed to work, but called off in the process. I followed the same route in my car, but instead of turning into my worksite, I kept going until I found the nearby gas station.

I pulled into my usual spot, shakingly inhaling a smoke as I looked at the field of corn surrounding it. The power line stood tall, almost menacing in the dark swirl of gloom in the sky.

It has to stop. *It has to.*

I snubbed out my cigarette and exited my car, feeling the chilly wind assault me as I closed the door behind me. I thought of calling the police, but I didn't know what I would tell them. Every scenario I imagined ended with me just being called crazy.

My feet moved on their own, and I swallowed hard as I started walking in the direction I had watched so many times on my lunch break. The grass faded and the corn began, and I made my way into the deafening sea of husks ahead. The stalks were loud and cracked under my feet, and the mud sucked at my shoes. I tripped and stumbled on the uneasy ground, and I grabbed the stalks in an attempt to keep myself balanced.

My legs burned and the crops scratched and whipped at me. Soon I felt lost in the corn, every step closing me off from the outside world. The corn stalks were taller the more you went in, until eventually I felt like I was being swallowed by it.

I kept my eyes on the power line above. I decided I would look there, and if I found nothing I would turn back and go back home. Maybe then I would get help.

Just as I was getting used to the crunch of my footsteps, the ground started to even out and I found myself in a small clearing. Four large metal posts stood on each side, posted at each corner of the clearing. I could hear the creak of metal swaying in the wind, and I felt myself shrink as I looked up.

I was standing underneath the power line now, next to the leg where I had first seen the skinned man a few days ago.

It was eerily quiet and cold in the clearing, moss and dead grass covering the churned mounds left behind by excavation. I felt the strong urge to run back to my car, but every time I closed my eyes I was reminded by the same piercing stare and scream. If I went back home, I would just go back to hiding in my apartment.

I looked for disturbed dirt, for a grave, for a body. What I found was nothing but cold dirt and dried husks, with the occasional rock jutting from the earth. I didn't know what I expected to find, but I found no skinned man, or signs of there ever being one. The corn swayed in the circle around the clearing, and I felt foolish for wandering out here by myself.

The wind picked up, and above the power line creaked. I watched the electrical lines sway in the sky, and I felt small and out of my depth. What was I hoping to find here? A skeleton laying in the grass?

Stupid, I thought to myself. Walking all the way out here, with not even as much as a shovel. My hands started to ache from the cold, and I found myself shivering. There was nothing to be found here. Maybe I *did* need help after all.

I turned around to leave, my cheeks burning with frustration. I felt my eyes water, the helpless draw of tears ready to further my own embarrassment.

There is no skinned man. You're just crazy. You're fuckin' crazy.

As I sulked back to the edge of the clearing, something caught my foot. I tripped and stumbled into the mud, looking back at whatever had a hold on me. It was heavy and cold, and it kicked up a line of dirt in its wake.

It was a metal chain.

I looked at it dumbfounded, the links heavily rusted and caked with dirt. I untangled my foot, then followed the mysterious chain toward its source. I got back on my feet and gathered the slack, staring at it for a moment before tugging on it. The lead disappeared into the earth in front of me, directly under the power line.

The chain was cold to the touch, but I wrapped it around my hands and started to pull. The earth fought against me, matted weeds and mud slinging as I ripped it from the ground. I pulled and pulled, digging my heels into the ground as I yanked it free. It caught suddenly, and I put all of my weight behind it, running backwards until it suddenly broke loose. In an uproar of debris, I felt flat on my ass.

And in front of me, a wooden door flung open.

A whisper cooed from underground, and I climbed to my feet and walked to it. It was the entrance to a dark pit, a crude ladder leading the way to an unseen destination. My mind begged to call the police; my body pleaded to go home. In the end I did neither, and my shoes soon found the rungs of the old forgotten ladder. The light above shows a floor of damp dirt and bones, long decayed and hidden in the dark.

The passage wasn't as long as I thought. It went down about ten feet, and I expected it to open up into some grand chasm below. But when the ladder came to an end, I found only a corridor, a ten-by-ten room carved deep into the earth. The light from above pooled in, cutting through a haze of dust and stagnant air. I squinted through the heavy particles, in an attempt to see what the light seemed to be *avoiding*. Once the dust began to fade, I could hear the whispers growing, a hushed chorus that called to me from the corner of the derelict hole.

The walls are etched with erratic text, words toppling words in an indecipherable message. I want to read the words, but I'm drawn away, my focus pulled to the corner where the light shines the least.

In the corner is a brass chair, and sitting in it, a corpse with dozens of limbs. I wanted to look away, but I couldn't, the mummified curled hands demanding my attention. It looked like a human, its skeletal frame filling the entirety of its throne-like seat. Empty eyes and a hanging mouth, its extra bony arms fanning out like wings. A gaping hole sits in the center of its chest, like something had been ripped out of it. Impossibly proportioned and long dead, the being dedicated several appendages to the object it held in its lap

.

A glass orb, radiating the slightest shimmer of red. The whispers were coming from it.

I remember being unable to lift my eyes from the orb. It drew me in, its whispers beckoning me to the dying glow it held within. The corpse stayed frozen in place, its decayed frame getting larger the closer I got. It wanted me to take the orb. It was offering it to me.

I reached out and touched it, a static aura tickling my fingers as they drew near the glass. I wanted the orb. I *needed* to hold it. Nothing else seemed to matter. My fingers hovered around the glass in anticipation, and a strange heat billowed from it as I prepared to lift it. I looked into the corpse's eyes, twin skeletal voids that watched from its petrified husk. Just as I grabbed the orb, the corpse's jaw clacked.

The orb exploded with red light, and with it, and unimaginable heat. The red glow consumed me like a raging fire, engulfing me until it covered my entire body. I tried to swipe it off of me, but it started to burn, a wicked chemical boil that seeped into my arms and legs like acid. I watched in horror as my skin started to part with me, bubbling and oozing until I was left with nothing but bloody meat. It collected and twisted in front of me like paint, a writhing mass that slipped through my fingers when I tried to grab at it. My strength began to fade, and my legs no longer felt capable of holding me.

I collapsed helplessly to the ground, glaring at the orb in betrayal as it shined bright and decadent. My muscles felt the pain of every speck of dirt, every piece of gravel that scraped mercilessly into my exposed flesh. The pain was unbearable, a never-ending scream across my entire body.

The mass of skin contorted and flexed, stretching across the corpse and its many limbs. It webbed between every finger and over every dried tendon, new life taking shape and cracking as it coated over the nightmarish husk. The arms, so many arms, assisted in the new fitting, pulling and tugging until the garb was complete. I could only reach out in my misery while it repaired itself, the horrible form worsening the longer I watched it mold.

Joints popped to life. Thin eyelids blinked. Once the form was complete, the gaping chest cavity quivered in agitation. Before my unclosable eyes, the being picked up the orb with its many hands and buried it into its chest. The cavity sealed on its own, tendrils of thin skin stitching itself until the red glow was no more.

While I lay helpless on the cold and painful dirt, the being rose from the chair, standing and stretching tall before hunching over on its multiple limbs. It looks at me for a moment, and emotionless clacking echoing in the chamber before it makes its way to the ladder, and climbs it like a spider. The last I see of the monstrosity is its appendages slinking into the light, right before the door slams shut behind it.

I've been in this darkness ever since. I don't know how long I've been down here. Hours, days, weeks. All I know is my constant suffering, and my inability to escape it. Despite my exposed body, I am immune to the cold, immune to the prospect of perishing.

That's not the only change. Since discovering the corpse, I can feel an extension of myself, an ethereal tether that lets me move beyond my miserable form on this cold earth. Some kind of drift between time and space. I don't know if it's an aftereffect of the orb itself, or my fractured sanity in this tomb I've found myself in. I can do other small things, like move grains of dirt or sway the air in one way or another. In an attempt to recollect some of my sanity I have inscribed my story on the walls of this grave, but the longer time goes on, the foggier the memories seem to get.

I don't understand it. I can only hope what I think is transpiring is real and not a fabrication of my delusional misery. I can't go far, but each time I find I can get a little further. I can see the cornfield above my tomb. I can almost feel the air dancing across it. If I focus hard enough... I can see myself. I don't know why they are there, or if it's even real. But if I try hard enough... maybe I could reach them.

I need to warn them and tell them to stay away from here. I need to warn them of the monster I set free. I don't know what it wants or why it was down here, but I fear for the life I left behind above ground. Maybe someone can stop it. Maybe *I* can stop it.

In my shattered mind, I remember where I used to work, where I used to live. If I can find them at the right time... maybe I can warn them. Maybe I can save them from a demise such as this.

THE FLOATING DOG

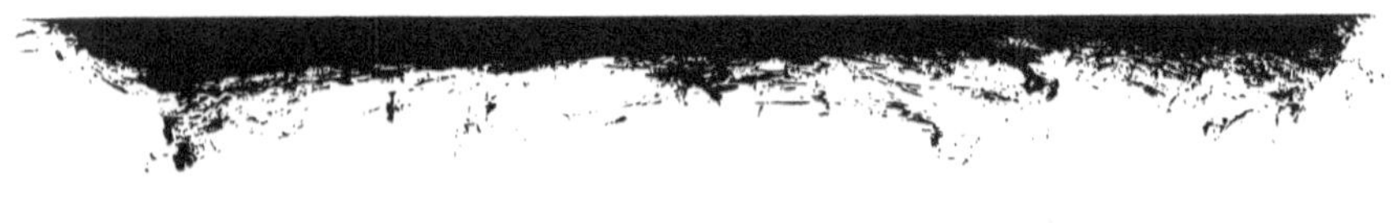

I eat lunch in the park every day. I take the elevator down, exit the lobby, and walk to whatever food truck is parked on the corner. Sometimes it's a hot dog, other times it's street tacos.

Once I buy my food, I like to go and sit at the park and eat. There's a fountain in the middle and a jogging trail that circles around it. On the days it's busy it's nice to sit and people watch, on the days it's not I scroll through my phone to kill time while I enjoy the breeze.

Parents pushing strollers, men and women jogging in spandex. Sometimes the pigeons bounce over and I toss them bits of my hotdog bun or tortilla, or the last of my fries. It's been pretty peaceful, aside from the guy I saw two days ago.

A homeless man running in the park, shouting at everyone around him. His commotion seemed to make everyone uneasy, heads turning and watching him flail at seemingly nothing. People sort of turned the other cheek and ignored him, as it wasn't entirely uncommon in the big city. A couple close by on a bench paused their chat over coffee for a moment, before disregarding him completely. In the end he ran away, his *help me's* echoing until he was out of sight. I tossed my scraps to the pigeons and returned to work. Back through the lobby, back up the elevator. Back to work.

Yesterday, I did the same as usual. Same regime down to get food—a deluxe hot dog today—with the poppy seed bun and a huge pickle. Like a salad bar and link on a bun. I sat on the bench like usual. There weren't many people out, so I settled into the bench, took a messy bite of my lunch, and started scrolling through social media.

"Oh god, oh god, someone help me please—"

I heard it coming from behind me, an approaching whimper that approached so fast, it startled me. A blur rushed past me and knocked me in the elbow. My lunch tumbled onto the dirty concrete, a sight that made the pigeons take notice.

A woman ran past me and into the park, huffing and crying, tears streaming down her face. There wasn't really anyone around, and those that saw her made an effort to ignore her. With hands squeezed into fists, she let out a panic cry, looking to anyone for help. She whirled around, and I felt my stomach twist when she saw me. She must not have even noticed me sitting there, despite ruining my lunch.

"Y-you! You gotta help me! It's coming" she shouted, begging me to come closer. Her hair was a mess, but she didn't look home-less, she just looked desperately out of breath.

Sitting on the bench, I look at her reluctantly. I looked at my lunch on the ground, then swiveled on the bench to look behind me.

There was nobody there, just your average busy street. No one giving chase, no one even really saw her. I turned around and saw the chubby little birds had already swarmed my food.

"What's coming?" I called to her awkwardly, seeing nothing but hungry pigeons.

She looked at me incredulously.

"Are you fucking kidding me? Look at it! *Look!*" She pointed desperately, starting to sob. I started to feel anxious, and I turned to look again.

There was nothing chasing her. Nothing at all.

I heard sirens in the distance, and the busy horns of traffic. There was nothing to see.

"I'm sorry, I don't know how to help you. You want me to call the police?" I sat up from the bench and offered my phone.

She just shook her head, her lip trembling. She started backing away.

"Miss?" I called out to her.

A jogger came around the corner in bright green spandex, air-pods stuck in his ears. She reached for him and touched his shoulder.

He flinched away, waving her off and saying something like "I don't have any money".

She looked past me, a look of utter defeat as she kept backing away. I looked the same direction, wanting to help—but there was nothing there. Nobody lingering behind a tree, or creeping after her.

"Oh god. I'm going to die. I'm going to die," she was saying.

"Miss, let me help you," I said, heading towards her, "here, I'll call the police. I'll stay with you until they—"

"NO! I *can't* stay. I have to go now. It's too close!"

Then she was gone, running in the same fashion the homeless man had the day before.

Today, it was raining. I looked out at the weather and contemplated my lunch. I didn't want to get wet, but I really wanted to get out of the office. I decided to go. I grabbed my wallet and keys, and pulled on my jacket. I stepped into the elevator and rode down. I exited through the lobby and stepped out into the rain. There was a pretzel truck today, and I could already taste the salt and cheese.

I winced against the rain and ordered a giant pretzel. I paid the guy and waited patiently, looking at my bench from underneath the shelter of the food truck. It's empty, just like I expected. The park is empty, too. Except for something lying in the middle of the park. I couldn't quite see it, but I got the nagging feeling something wasn't right. Like it's a body.

"Hey man, you see that?" I asked the cook, and he leaned out the window to look.

"See what?" he asked impatiently, squinting to see through the rain.

"I don't know, man. It's green. *There.* You see it?" I asked, pointing directly at it.

"Nah, man," he said, and went about getting the pretzel ready.

I wanted to wait, but the eerie curiosity nagged at me. I left the food truck and crossed the street in the rain. I saw the shape clearer as I got close, and I started to feel sick.

There's no way, it couldn't be.

Rain hammered the fountain water and the stretch of grass before it. Slumped on their side off the running path is the jogger in green, their body still in the heavy rain. I approached cautiously, digging out my phone. Before I even saw him, I knew he was dead.

The jogger's eyes were lifeless, globes with the light sucked out of them. His mouth was open, and it looked like he was foaming at the mouth. I tried to shake him, but his body was solid and ice cold. Like he's been dead a while. Frozen.

Suddenly I got a searing, mind-splitting headache. Like my brain was being ripped apart. I cried out in pain, squeezing my eyes closed as I grabbed my head to try and ride out the pain. My knees buckled, and I fell next to the jogger, writhing on the ground in agony.

As quickly as it starts, the migraine blinks away. I sit up in the grass, water soaking through my pants and running down my face. My chest was heavy, and I gasped for breath, overcome with the relief that the pain has faded away.

When I looked at the ground next to me, I gasped.

The jogger is gone.

"What the ..." I looked around to see if anyone else saw it, but there was no one there. It was mind boggling, but bleeding into my confusion—was a gnawing, *primal* fear. I felt its presence before I saw it, and when I did, I felt my breath being ripped from my lungs.

There was a faint ringing in my ears, one I could tell was getting louder as it got closer.

An unexplainable horror in both its appearance and its movement. I watched it approach from across the park, a slow glide that seemed to be homing in where I was standing.

It was a floating dog, dead from the looks of it. It was standing up straight, its hind legs dangling perfectly still just inches above the ground. Its paws were aimed straight out like they were posed, like a real-life model of something that didn't render properly. Blood dripped down the sharp teeth of its bottom jaw, trickling down a red stain that's soaked into its fur. The top jaw is missing completely, like it broke off half of its skull.

Just seeing it makes me scream. I started to move, and it turned just slightly, adjusting its path so it would eventually meet me. Even with it so far away, I could *smell* it. A putrid gagging smell of death, decay, and festering maggots.

I shouted again, but there was no one to hear me. I panicked and ran across the street, cars blasting their horns as they halted right before me. I yelled and rambled at them, and they waved me furiously off the road.

When I looked back, it was following. The same slow glide, paws pointing towards me. Standing perfectly still, even as it started *clipping* through the passing cars. It stopped for nothing.

The man at the pretzel truck was irritated, still holding the order for me. He cleared his throat to let me hear it, but I didn't even give him the chance.

"Help! You gotta help me! You see that? You see that thing following me?!" I cry, grabbing his arm and shaking him.

"C'mon, man—" he starts, but I beg him to look.

He looked down the sidewalk, where the floating dog was approaching. My ears rang, and I gagged against the smell, releasing a gurgle of vomit that splashed against the side of the food truck.

"Man, what the hell?! There's nothing there man, now get the fuck outta here!" He shouted angrily. I took off down the sidewalk.

It wouldn't stop for anything. The same eerie glide through the rain.

When I looked at it, I felt like I was going to die.

I ran down the street like a madman, asking every person that crossed my path. They didn't see the dog. Of course they didn't. They waved me off and pulled out their phones, offering to call the police or get me help or hand me money.

They couldn't see it. Nobody can see it.

Why won't it stop?

Why won't it stop following me?

* * *

I've been riding the subway for hours. I'm afraid to go home, afraid of what will happen when it catches me. I know it's out there. I don't want to see it. I'm scared to see it. But I'm so tired. I'm not sure how long I can keep running from it.

The subway rides on a loop across the entire city, and I paid to ride it through the night. I'm pretty sure I'm safe. For now, at least.

But every time I close my eyes, I catch a whiff of that horrible smell.

Only for a moment, and then it's gone.

MONA

I was longing for some spark in my life. I swiped on her on Tinder, tags like **"looking to try new things"**, **"soul-searching"** and **"adventurous"** setting off mini fireworks in my head. I had previously gotten out of a long-term relationship, one that ended as drawn-out and miserable as watching the family dog wither away. My ex had cheated on me, and once I rode out the tide of my grief, I was looking to get out there again.

Her name was Mona. Raven-black hair, pale skin covered in tattoos, eyes so hot they could start a fire. I knew she was out of my league... you could imagine my surprise when my swipe led to a match.

She messaged me not long after the fact. She was a woman who went after what she wanted, which was something I found very attractive. We messaged back and forth, something I had to reassure myself was really happening with how fucking hot she was. It didn't make any sense to me. We texted for a bit, and when we seemed to hit it off, we talked on the phone. Her voice was smooth as silk, and her compliments made my heart flutter. We talked for hours, and as we chatted into the night, we got to know more about each other.

I was a geek that spent the better part of my twenties tinkering with computers and coding websites. She was into cosplay, painting, and fucking in public.

She mentioned her interests nonchalantly, the last one taking me by surprise. It felt like a red flag, but I couldn't ignore the rush of blood it gave me in more places than one. She just sounded so *sweet* on the phone. I laughed it off and tried not to sound apprehensive about it. It *did* sound a little wild for me, but I wasn't stupid. She had to be a catfish, or after my credit card number. Part of me wanted to ditch the situation, but I couldn't help but think of her profile pictures.

She was a walking goddess, and 100% too beautiful to be hanging out with the likes of me. Not to mention, *probably* fake as fuck.

But if she wasn't...

We made plans to have coffee the next day. I figured if she was fake, it would be easy to pick up on, and I would just responsibly make an exit before I got scammed. I was caught between the dilemma of fucking over myself, or possibly fucking her.

The next day, we met at a local coffee shop. I couldn't believe when she actually walked in; her long black hair accented by a similar shade of sundress and flats. Skin pale as the moon, with some of the coolest tattoos I had ever seen. She was shy, walking in awkwardly. An awkwardness that seemed to melt away when she saw me.

It was probably the best date I'd ever had. It felt like love at first sight, some bullshit you'd see in the movies. Despite my apprehension, she was actually *real*, and unbearably adorable.

Our conversation was awkward and cheesy at first, but I soon found myself infatuated with her. I started to feel guilty, meeting her for coffee in hopes of a hookup. Her body was incredible, yes, but it wasn't her petite curves that started to make my heart race.

The twinkle she held in her eyes. The way she tucked her hair before each sip of coffee. The animated motions she made with her hands when she talked about herself. The way she caressed her arm when she talked about herself.

This woman wasn't just hot, she was *beautiful.*

We left the shop and decided to walk in the park, leaving the congested air for a fresh and flowing breeze. We talked about work, and day-to-day stress. She told me she was a social worker that focused on rehabilitation. She didn't elaborate much, only saying there was *more* to people than what meets the eye, and how most are often misunderstood. She told me stories of those she had worked with in the past, hopeless people that found faith in themselves and turned over a new leaf. It was astonishing, and through my amalgamation of infatuated lust, was a respect for her humble strife.

We came near a loop in the walking park, a spot where the concrete trail bordered a thick lush of woods. She remarked how it would be the perfect spot to slip away and relieve some stress. I felt nervous, and mentioned it felt like a little *much.* I liked her a lot, but it just felt so... *taboo.*

She kissed me then, and I'll never forget the softness of her lips. She told me it was okay to be scared, and she didn't want to rush me, *but* she wanted to show me how fun it could be. I looked into her sparkling eyes, and wondered how I, or *anyone,* could say no to just a taste.

We slinked away to the woods, deep enough to be out of obvious sight but close enough for the potential chance of being caught. I wasn't into it at first, but as her kisses grew more passionate, and her hand found its way into my jeans, I couldn't help but look at the walking path still in view, throbbing so hard it hurt.

Her breath was seductive in my ear, one hand feeling the strength of my arousal while the other guided my hand to her breast. I was soon caressing it eagerly, my thumb softly searching across the soft fabric of her dress. Once I no longer needed instruction to touch, she left my hand there and reached underneath her dress and between her legs. Her breathing slowed and her grip on me tightened. I looked cautiously to the walking path, where another couple was coming around, unbeknownst to us.

My heart raced, and I started to panic over being caught. The feeling melted away when I looked at Mona, her eyes closed as she started to disappear inside herself. I took it all in, hearing the increasing pace of her breathing, the wind on her hair, the porcelain skin of her neck and shoulders. Her lips parted in a whisper, and she asked me to finish for her.

I came harder than ever before. My view of the walking couple disappearing as my eyes involuntarily closed as I could only ride out the pulsating wave. Mona leaned against me as she got her own, and I was suddenly imprisoned in the agony of the moment. When it faded away, we looked at each other, the haze leaving us breathing hard and blushing. I looked into her twinkling eyes, and she smiled, I felt like a weight had been lifted.

This was the first of many risqué encounters. Aside from the whole "being in public" thing we *actually did* take it slow, if only for a moment. There were days, sometimes over a week, before we would meet up again, but it would always start the same. At least in the beginning.

Our next date ended in the same fashion, except instead of a stroll in the park after lunch, it ended in the parking lot outside the restaurant. Steam and kisses and my seat leaned back as she took me as far as she could down her throat. I listened to every exasperated suck of breath through the view of the bar and grill, people going about their meal without the inclination to look outside. Those who did didn't draw attention. The climax was just as good if not better than the last, my eyes forcing themselves to close again as she grabbed my hips and accepted everything. This time when I was finished, we changed places.

It was unreal, and I couldn't get enough. Mona made it clear that she didn't want a relationship. She just wanted to share these moments with me. Having left my long relationship before this, I agreed and just accepted the excitement while I had it.

The third was spent browsing the thrift store, deviously batting eyes at the changing room. Only to slip away and "relieve stress", taking in the advantages of platform boots and a mini-skirt while keeping an eye between the wooden slats of the changing stall door.

It wasn't the act of sex, but the thrill. A thrill we shared together, and all-or-nothing dice throw with the best possible payload. Muffling her breathing with a clasped hand and silencing my own against the shine of her black hair was better than any vanilla night out, and by the fourth I couldn't fathom how I lived without it for so long.

The fourth consisted of a night out at a fancy restaurant, only to call for the check early and hail a cab (despite driving there myself). The need to perform lost in front of a potential audience only seemed to get worse with each consecutive time, as did the arousal.

Despite her name, Mona was a silent lover. But she was giving, every time trying to coax what she could out of me as quickly as possible. Her anticipation of the finish was hungry, *greedy* even, and she would feed off visible and audible cues to further propel herself to her own eruption. It was something I just couldn't get enough of, like I had to starve in the days between it took until the next meet. But just as strong as the rush came to be, the abrupt clarity was tenfold.

Part of me wanted to stop. But I never did.

Even when I locked eyes with the cab driver in the rear-view mirror, stiffening as Mona collected everything on top of me. Grabbing fistfuls of my shirt as she pulled me closer, all I could do was watch the poor guy look away in discomfort. The thought of putting on a free show was suddenly replaced by a heavy veil of shame. Only to be dropped off at my apartment like it never happened.

I felt like I was going downhill, and I couldn't stop it.

Tossing and turning through the night alone, somehow still finding the nag of arousal when I close my eyes. Nightmares of eyes watching behind the pale silhouette of perfect curves and silent agony. Then waking up alone, sad and uncomfortably stiff. The shame was still there when I woke up, like a lingering haze, much unlike the powerful wave granted from the public fuck.

I didn't know what the hell was happening to me. I looked in the mirror and hardly recognized myself. In the dragging hours of my free time, all I can think about is when I can go again.

Which brings me to today. Or earlier, I guess. Usually I have to wait a couple days before hearing from Mona again, but today she texted me for a follow up the next day. This time, she wanted me to go to *her* place. To make **a movie.**

It hadn't dawned on me that I didn't know where she lived until she texted me the address. I don't know why, but I had a bad feeling about going. Like if I went out, I would be making a grave mistake. My mind seemed to conflict against itself, trying to decipher the proper course of action moving forward.

In the end, I grabbed my keys and headed for the door, freshly showered and groomed. The undying arousal was evident, despite the sick feeling that was brewing in my stomach. I started my car and left, heading for the destination I programmed into my GPS.

Mona lived on the outskirts of town, in a nice country home with lots of land. It looked like a nice place for peace and quiet, the entire property closed off by a thick forest as far as the eye could see. I parked and sat at the wheel for a moment, taking a look at the sky.

There was a full moon, and basking in the glow was Mona, waiting for me, leaning against her car. I got out of the car, and she greeted me, a quick embrace with a peck on the cheek. She was wearing a black silk nightgown, a lack of undergarments immediately apparent with how thin the fabric was. She wore no make-up or jewelry, and I realized this was probably the purest I had seen her yet. No bells or whistles, just a thin layer of silk.

She led me by the hand, excitingly taking me to the back-yard.

"We're not doing it inside?" I asked, nervously.

"No. I have the perfect scene set for us. *In the middle of the woods.* I've always wanted to do it, and the moon is perfect. I have everything set up there," she said, quickening her pace.

I thought of the concept, going at it in the moonlight in front of a camera. It sounded creepy, but the more I thought it over, the more alluring it felt. I followed behind her, looking down her back to her accented curves, to the faint reflection of her bare feet. I was starting to feel overdressed.

I looked at her house as we passed it; each window was dark and ominous like there was nobody home. The paint was peeling, and the shingles looked battered, like there hadn't been any upkeep in a decade. It looked like no one even lived there.

"Eyes on me, handsome. You're not getting cold feet, are you?" she teased, tugging me along.

"Nope. I'm good," I said, anxiously watching the approaching tree line. It was starting to feel chilly, but Mona didn't seem to mind.

We slipped into the trees much like we did on our first date, but I couldn't see much of anything. We talked a little about the film she wanted to make, one she planned on uploading to a few of the major pornographic websites. I mentioned I wasn't sure if I wanted to have my face in it, and she assured me that she had prepared for that, and everything would be taken care of.

I thought of one of those little masquerade masks, and it actually sounded silly and fun. I thought of the people who would click on the video, and for some reason the thought of other people getting off on our thrill filled me with an excitement just as pure and surprising as our first stint in the bushes at the walking park. I felt the rush of blood, and my pants seemed unbearably tight. Mona noticed my excitement and ran the back of her hand against it.

Mona led me to a blanket in the middle of the woods, one positioned where the ground seemed the most accommodating. The moon came through the treetops in bright slits, each of them shining on the blanket. Laying on the blanket was a goat mask, one that actually kind of made me jump once my eyes registered it. In front of it was a nice-looking camera on a tripod. There was nothing but dark trees surrounding us, and the eeriness started to hamper my erection.

When we got to the blanket, Mona immediately started to undress me, unbuttoning my shirt and tugging it from the waistband of my jeans. The air was chilly, and I tried to hype myself up by running my hand underneath her nightgown, but I felt like I couldn't grasp the spark.

"What's with the mask?" I said, gesturing to it on the blanket.

"I thought you didn't want your face in it?" she said, pulling my jeans down to expose my briefs.

"Well, yeah, but I thought maybe it would be something like—" I started, and she put a finger to my lips.

"Shhhhh. This is a fantasy of mine, don't *ruin* it. Plus, the algorithm will love it," she said, grabbing it from the blanket. She handed it to me and reached inside my underwear. Her hands were cold, but still amazingly soft. She worked my courage up with slow strokes and whispered in my car.

"Put it on. I'm ready for you now,"

I did as I was told, pulling on the creepy goat mask before stripping the rest of my clothes. The mask smelt like clammy prophylactic, like it had been sitting in an attic for years. Mona turned the camera on, a little red eye blinking before she got on her hands and knees on the blanket, offering herself to me.

I'll spare you the exact words of her command, but I definitely obeyed. The ground was hard and uneven, my knees pressing into exposed roots in the earth. I pulled back the veil gently, and watched the moon reflect off her perfect, tattooed skin. Seeing it ready for me dissipated my nerves, and once I felt her slickness, I couldn't go back.

I entered harder than I planned, but I didn't regret it. The collision of my hips on her soft skin brought the blanket into fistfuls in her delicate fingers immediately, and I took the cue that she wasn't looking for a buildup. Our encounters were usually quick, but this time I actually had to stifle myself to ruin it early. When I tried to restrain myself, Mona backed into encouragingly, the softest whisper of ecstasy escaping her usually quiet agony.

In no time at all, I was huffing behind the mask, watching her fall more and more apart through the small openings that I imagined were on the bridge of the goat's nose. She was really into what we were doing, and it drove me wild. I kept feeling the taunted buildup of my own pleasure, and found myself repeatedly slowing down to reign it back in. After the fourth time, Mona decided to take matters into her own hands.

She pulled off of me and pushed me to the ground, climbing on top before I could even situate comfortably. Once I was reinserted, she leaned back and took it all, pausing only to let the nightgown fall from her shoulders. She bathed in the moonlight, looking just like the goddess I felt she was.

She started to ride, *hard.* I looked up at her from behind the mask, my own condensating breath huffing harder and harder as she tried to push me over the edge. I looked from her beautiful exposure to the red eye of the camera, and for a moment I wished this encounter could've stayed just between us. It just felt so *right,* I wanted to selfishly cherish it.

Mona tried harder and harder to provoke my climax, rocking her hips and taking me as deep as she could through her repetitive squeezes. She looked like she didn't have long left herself.

After riding the edge for the dozenth time, I decided it was time to give her what she wanted. Without a word, I reached up and grabbed her by the shoulders, pulled her close, and started doing the work. She collapsed and embraced me tightly, riding out her apex as I pushed us to the summit with my hips from below. I could barely breathe behind the mask, and I closed my eyes to push through the exhaustion to get us past the finish line.

I listened to Mona come undone on top of me, the muffled *mmf-mmf-mmf* of her silent moans breathing into my neck as I increased the pace. Just as I was ready to selfishly explode, I heard something that made me pull away from the climax. Through Mona's heavy breathing, I heard... someone *else's* breathing.

My eyes shot open in their plastic prison, trying to squint while I reeled back from the edge. I looked over Mona's shoulders and saw nothing at first, the images slowly trying to refocus through the encroaching orgasm. Then I looked past the camera, and locked eyes with it.

Almost out of view was someone on their knees, their mouth duct-taped and their hands bound with rope. They looked terrified, tears streaming down their face as a hand firmly grasped their shoulder. Standing next to them was a tall figure in a red robe, their face featureless save for wide lidless eyes and a horribly broken jaw. Next to them was another, then another, then...

The closest robed figure reached into their shawl and produced a curved silver dagger, one they ran straight into the throat of the person on their knees. *Repeatedly.*

"Oh fuck, what the fffff—" I bucked and tossed Mona off of me, and started to backwards crawl into the leaves. I pulled the slimy goat mask off and whipped my head around, suddenly seeing the shapes of at least twenty robed individuals.

"Wait, no," Mona started, reaching for me.

"No, what the fuck, *what the fuck*—" I shouted deliriously, my eyes locking once again with the person being stabbed.

The robed figure ran the knife in again, and a wet gurgle echoed from the poor captive as they started to choke on their own blood. The robed figure made them look at me, even as their life started fading.

"*Don't go.* We're so close. We need this. *I* need this," Mona begged, a hidden anger rising in her sweet, catching breath. It wasn't until then that I saw it, the spool of rope, roll of duct-tape, and a dagger of her own next to the blanket.

I stared at all of them, Mona and her pale nakedness, the men in robes staring with menacing, bloodshot eyes. I wanted to say something, something meaningful, but in the end, I just screamed like a panic-stricken lunatic.

I scrambled to my feet and started to run, only having time to grab my pants and leaving everything else behind me. I screamed again as I bumped into another robed figure. One had been watching from behind the whole time and was now grabbing at me with gnarled, bony fingers. I ran past them, screaming as I went, my meat flopping painfully against my thighs as I ran scared.

I made it through the backyard, the sound of Mona's shouts echoing as my eyes met my car in the driveway. My keys jingled in the pocket of my jeans, and I will forever be thankful that I grabbed them instead of my shirt. Completely naked and horrified, I turned the car on and floored it, angling the car awkwardly in a swerve through the front yard. I only got a glimpse of Mona and her subordinates emerging from the trees before I was peeling back out onto the road.

I called the police and explained what had happened, and they instructed me to head to the station while they sent a unit to the address I provided. I spent the entire drive looking in the rear-view mirror, expecting those ghastly bloodshot eyes to be gaining on me, but I never saw them.

Arriving at the police station with nothing but jeans was awkward, but they were thankfully understanding. They questioned me thoroughly about what happened, and I gave them the same uneasy story multiple times. The police took the number and ran it, and it doesn't belong to anybody. There's no phone records.

They got me some clothes and water, and I stayed there until after they sorted it out. Hours later, a unit called in and said they searched the perimeter and found no one inside the house. Apparently it was abandoned and hadn't had an owner in over a decade.

When they searched the woods, they found no robed figures, no dead body, no Mona.

Only a bloodstain of heavy arterial spray.

I'm in a hotel now. I'm too scared to go home. I don't know if they'll find me there. I've just been sitting on the bed, scrolling through the texts left on my phone from Mona.

Looking to try new things.

Soul-searching.

Adventurous.

What the fuck. I close my eyes, and all I see is the haunted vision of that poor person duct-taped and tied up. That and the glaring red dot of the camera recording me.

I flinch at every creak in the night, and panic when my phone goes off. She hasn't tried to contact me.

Worst of all... I miss Mona.

FALSE FACE

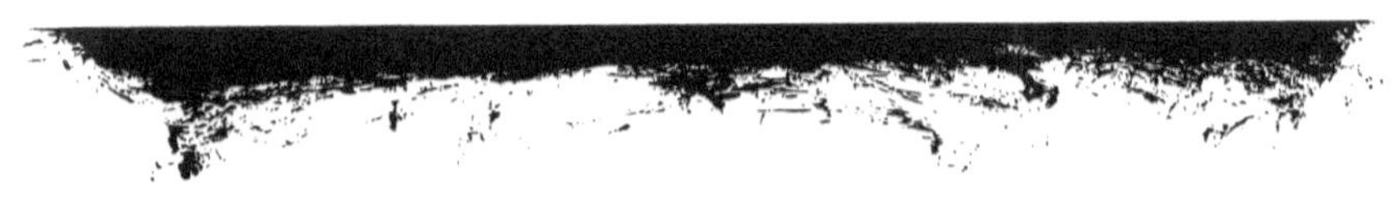

I was there when he bought the damn thing. We went to a garage sale just out of town; an old woman's house that had the driveway filled to the very edge with hand-me-downs and knick-knacks. My sister Angie and I were waving through a selection of old dresses when he surprised us with it.

He was just standing there, staring at us behind the eyeholes of that hideous thing. I'll never forget that thousand-yard stare, coupled with those unsettling lips and wispy strands of hair. I nearly jumped out of my skin, and my sister screamed, one that drew the attention of everyone else browsing the drive.

It was just a prank, something Tom was known for, but there was something so awful about that mask. It looked like a human face.

"You're such a dick!" Angie said, flailing at his chest. He laughed for a second, extending his arms and acting like a zombie, cheesy moans and all. He kept laughing as he pulled it off, the stretch of the thin rubber elongating the nose and cheeks.

"I'm sorry! I couldn't resist. I mean, *look* at this thing!" Tom said as he hugged her around the waist playfully, holding it out for her to see. She was flustered and holding back tears, but she tried to play it off.

"*Thanks.* I hate it," Angie said, pushing it away.

I knew then she *really* didn't like it. Angie was sensitive to pranks like that. Even when we were kids, she would bawl every time I would hide somewhere and scare her, crying long after our parents would comfort her. It was something that stuck with her even into our college years. Angie *hated* to be scared.

Tom stopped laughing, sensing he had clearly hit a nerve.

"Alright babe, I'm sorry. *Sorry,* okay? I'll put it back," he said, attempting to soothe her with a caress on her cheek. One she didn't give into until after he tossed it back in the box he found it in. It rolled sloppily over some old VHS tapes, coming to a flattened halt on its side. The empty eye holes stared innocently at Angie, and she shuddered as they went back to browsing.

The mask seemed to have a personality of its own. It was fucking creepy, plain and simple. I knew the thing was going to be a problem, so as they walked away, I tried to hide it. I covered it up with another box, one filled with weathered basketballs and old tennis rackets. Tom was smart, even going to college to be a doctor. But he was a natural prankster. If he found it again, he wouldn't be able to stop himself from buying it.

Not long after, we concluded our day at the garage sale. We got a pretty good haul, I found a few old sweaters that would look good with some shoes I had, and Angie got a pair of platform boots, as well as an old vinyl of *Purple Rain.*

Tom got a haul of his own, clutching an old paper grocery filled with jeans and a 90's version of the *Ab-coaster.*

Together, we left the garage sale and headed back to town. I drove, and Angie sat up front with me. Tom sat in the backseat, rifling through his bag to inspect the jeans he bought, mumbling something like "you have to pay to get them like this now."

We drove for a while, taking back roads on our return to town so we could enjoy the sun and the weather. Things had gotten so busy as we got older, it was nice to just drive around like we did when we were teenagers. Looking back, I wish I had taken more time to enjoy Angie's company and make more effort to hang out outside of work.

By the time we got to town, we decided we would grab something to eat. We pulled into a burger place, intending to get some food and eat outside. As I swung into a parking spot, Angie unbuckled her seatbelt and swiveled in her seat. I saw it coming in the rear-view mirror, but it was too late.

The scream that followed could've woken the dead.

Tom was sitting perfectly still in the backseat. Stretched across his face was the mask from the garage sale.

Angie ran out of the car, screaming bloody murder. Tom took the mask off immediately and threw his hands up in surrender, but Angie was *inconsolable.*

"I didn't actually buy it, it was just there in the bag."

"I don't know how it came with me, *I swear.*"

"You saw me buy my stuff! I didn't buy it. I didn't even know where it was!"

"I don't know why I put it on. I just thought I'd get you one more time. I'm sorry. I don't know why I did it."

Tom pleaded his case, but ultimately it was his fault for buying it, even more so for putting it back on. I didn't actually see him buy it, but he was smart enough to figure out a way to hide it.

In the end, I was the only one to calm her down. Sprinkling some of that older-sister charm, in the midst of the shitty looks I gave Tom.

He gave me the mask, and I threw it in the trash. I told him I'd kill him if he scared my sister like that again. He apologized several times, most of which fell on deaf ears. He said the same thing over and over again.

I promise I'll never put the mask on again. It's gone, okay? It's over. I promise.

I could hear the sincerity in his voice, he understood he fucked up.

But all I could see was the unsettling look of his eyes behind the mask in the rear-view mirror. I wasn't easily scared, but there was just something not right about that mask. It made me think of a woman's face.

Angie came around, eventually. Tom paid for our meals in an attempt to make amends, but it was pretty clear he was in the doghouse for the rest of the day. We ate our food in silence, Angie sniffling while she chewed her cheeseburger. Tom tried joking and turning on the charm. It worked a little bit, but you could tell she was still wounded over the ordeal.

After we ate, we decided it was time to call it a day and return home. The two of them had school in the morning, and I had to work the next day. I made an effort to check the garbage before I left. The mask was still there, quietly watching underneath burger wrappers and fountain cups. It stayed there as we pulled away. Tom didn't even look at it.

They sat together in the backseat, and Angie warmed up to him again. They talked about school, trending shows, and current events. They laughed. Tom was funny when he wanted to be, and he could be really sweet when he wasn't fucking around. I don't think I'd ever fully forgive him for the second scare. You don't quite forget something like that.

Before I got to the campus, they were sweet on each other again, and I had to tell them to "get a room". They laughed a little. It seemed like they had gotten past it.

Tom's dorm was a couple miles away, and my sister's apartment was only a couple blocks down the road from there. It was dusk by the time I dropped them off. We said our goodbyes and made plans to get together again when things got less busy, on the condition that we wouldn't go to any garage sales next time.

On the way home, I thought of that horrible mask, and how bad it had scared Angie. There was something about it that I just couldn't shake. The way its dingy locks felt like human hair. The way the rubber felt like *real skin.*

Even as I dozed off to a show, I couldn't get the image out of my head. It made me want to drive back to that burger joint, dig it out of the trash and set it on fire.

In the middle of the night, I woke to the sound of my phone going off. Through the fog of sleep, I checked the time. It was shortly after 2am. Angie was calling me.

I answered immediately, thinking something was wrong.

"Hey, Ang. What's going on?" I said through a yawn.

There was nothing on the other line for a time, and I wondered if she had called me on accident.

"Ang? You there? Hello?"

The only response was rapid breathing, like someone was running in the background.

"Hello? *Angie,* you there?"

She hung up. I immediately called back.

The phone just rang on the other end, over and over until her voicemail picked it up. I left a message telling her I was worried, and for her to call back.

I was just about to set the phone down and go back to sleep, when I realized I had some unseen notifications. Like a lot of them.

Angie had texted me several times, more and more frequently leading up to her call:

> Hey, you up?

> I know it's stupid, but I keep thinking about that mask

> You guys threw it away right?

Right?

I called Tom, but he's not answering. Probably playing cod again :/

You guys threw it away right?

Sorry, I can't stop thinking about it. I know it's dumb

Wtf

We lost power, weird

Tom's not answering, would you mind picking me up? I can't sleep

I guess I'll just try to sleep. It's fuckin creepy here though

I think there's someone in my apartment

Oh god

The last text was an attachment, an image that hadn't downloaded yet. My heart raced as I stared at the screen, waiting for the Wi-Fi to do its thing.

When I opened the image, I wanted to scream.

The picture looked like her living room, the center of it illuminated by the flash of her phone's camera. Tom was sitting on the couch in the dark, staring blankly at the turned off television. He was only wearing a t-shirt and boxers, his feet covered in dirt.

Stretched over his head was that horrible mask.

I called Angie again, and when she didn't pick up, I called the police. I reported a break-in, and started getting dressed to head over there myself.

By the time I arrived, the entire apartment complex was lit up. Four squad cars, a firetruck, and an ambulance. No sign of Angie, or Tom. Neither of them answered the phone.

People were standing outside in their pajamas, looking terrified, pointing their fingers. I had to push past the group to see, and when I did, I felt a knot forming in my throat. Everyone was looking at the same thing, despite the policemen's efforts to keep them back.

The stairs leading to Angie's apartment were covered in blood, a trail that continued onto the sidewalk and into the grass. The messy drag mark kept going until it reached the woods, where it seemingly vanished.

It took two weeks before the police would give me any details, aside from what I already knew. They can't really explain what happened, and they don't really have a straight answer. There's obvious suspicion of foul play, but there's no witnesses. With the power being out, there's no eyewitness statement on what unfolded. They suspect the blood spatter started in the bedroom, but there's no murder weapon to clarify exactly what happened. There's dozens of handprints on the sheets, stained in blood. All Angie's, because they're simply too small for a man's hands. There were muddy footprints all over her apartment, but only an adult male's. Angie didn't take another step after what happened in the bed.

They're saying it's almost like she just... mutilated herself.

They searched the woods for her, but the trail went cold immediately. No blood after the drag mark... nothing. Like they just disappeared.

Tom didn't have a car. That night, he had left his phone, wallet, and dorm key on his nightstand.

They said they'll keep me updated, but I can see it in their eyes. They have nothing. It's already over.

I went back to that burger joint where we tossed the mask and went through the garbage. I checked the bin we tossed it in, even cut open every bag in the dumpster behind the building. The mask wasn't there.

I went to the old woman's house and questioned her about the mask she sold us, but she had no idea what I was talking about. She remembered us quite clearly, but she said she never sold us a mask. She never *had* one in the first place.

Both Angie and Tom were never seen again.

Their disappearance and the cause have shaken our little town to its core. I don't understand. Nobody seems to understand. The news can speculate, people can form their "theories", but it doesn't really matter.

The lack of reasoning behind this isn't what keeps me up at night. It's not the fact that the trail goes cold. It's not the fact that we combed the woods and found nothing, not a single trace of where they had gone. Or the fact that the burger joint was three and a half miles away from the dorms and her apartment—nearly seven there and back. It's a little detail in the police report, one that was left out of the press.

Tom's muddy footprints were all over the crime scene. Up the apartment stairs, heavy imprints outside the door before they let themselves in. They led from the front door to the couch, where he sat in the same spot of the picture Angie sent me. A single path leads to the bedroom, presumably following her to the bedroom where she ran in fear. The mud tracks don't follow her to the bed, though.

They go up the wall and onto the ceiling, where they stop. Directly above her bed.

Like he just stood there and watched her from above.

In the exact spot I see them now.

LAYING IN THE SHOWER

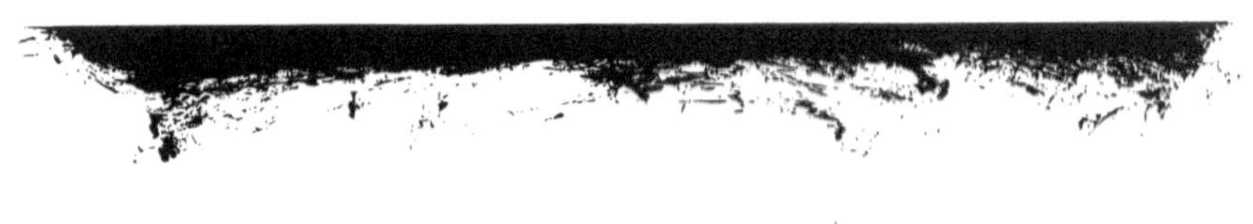

I drank too much. Again.

The only conceivable solace I could find in my extremely hungover state came in the form of steam and scalding water, and I indulged in the only way I thought possible: laying in the shower.

Thoughts of the night before come and go through the lens of a broken kaleidoscope, each drink remembered with a punishing throb from the inside of my skull. I'd like to say I was celebrating, going out on the town with friends or participating in some kind of party. The truth is, this is just the latest stunt in my own shameful self-indulgence. Like the ones before, I *swear* it's the last time. Deep down, I know I'm only lying to myself.

I don't know how long I've been here. My only keeper of time is the slowly cooling temperature of the water, one I ignore by slowly turning the knob further with my foot. I don't think of the added money on the energy bill or the wasted time of my day off, my only concern is the soothing water that berates me, and the muggy air with each labored breath.

I live alone. No significant other. No kids.

While I'm happy there's no one to see me like this, a part of me wishes there was. Someone to judge my decisions, maybe someone to encourage me to be better. Someone to help take this pain away.

Briefly, I open my eyes and look around my small enclosure in the shower. The beige vinyl covered in trickling water is somehow soothing, a silent comfort as I watch the mist collect on my skin. For a moment I look up at the shower head to see the continuous rain it bestows upon me. It's a cheap shower head; one of the streams sprays out of line, directly into the wall where a washcloth is hanging. The insignificant defection doesn't bother me, but it's soaked the rag fully, causing a repetitive drip that lands on the ledge of the tub. A *drip-drop* that annoyingly splashes my face.

My head throbs, my neck is stiff, and my blood pressure feels too high. I ignore the annoying splash from the washcloth and nestle back into the crook of my arm, trying to block out the memories of the night before, and the nights before that.

Just as I feel myself succumb to the dampened relaxation and fall asleep, I hear a noise.

A tapping.

I think I imagine it, so I ignore it. I stir uncomfortably, repositioning my face so water doesn't collect in my ear. I focus on the running water, hearing the rhythm of the shower's stream, with the occasional *drip-drop* of the soaked washcloth. I think of how I should've saved something from the night before, a little hair of the dog to ease the brunt of my ailments. If only I wasn't so damn self indulgent and didn't drink the last drop of everything I had.

I hear the tap again. Louder, this time.

I open my eyes, the weight of lead shutters lifting as I look around me. I see the shower walls and the trickling water. With an exasperated sigh, I shift and try to prop myself up to look around better, but each movement is taxing and feels like too much work. I poke my head past the shower curtain briefly and see the bathroom door still shut as I left it. The bathroom is empty, there's nobody there. Nothing but the haze of steam from the shower. I listen for the sound again, blinking away water that collects on my face.

For a time, there's nothing.

I lean forward and turn the knob on the faucet again, increasing the heat once more. It's feeling chilly, and I just want a little more time before I transition from here to my bed. As I sink back into the same awkward position, I hear it again. I feel an uncanny anxiety creep over me, followed by the scrawl of goosebumps.

It's coming from the wall in the shower.

I find myself sitting there, looking at the wall. I must be losing it. There's no way there could be anything there; behind the wall the shower is built into is just the walk-in closet of my bedroom. There's nothing in there but clothes and boxes.

I need to stop drinking, I think to myself.

I dismiss the noise and settle back in, resting my cheek in my elbow before closing my eyes. I focus on my breathing, the slow inhale and exhale of steam as I mentally find a better place. I focus on the water again, listening to the rhythmic stream followed by the drops from the hanging washcloth—

I hear the tap again. Louder than before.

The sound makes me jump, and I look around nervously. I subconsciously make a mental note of everything in the shower with me: vinyl surround with trickling water, a squeeze bottle of shampoo on the ledge next to me, a rounded bar of soap sitting dangerously close to the edge… everything seems in place. I listen for the noise, putting my hand on the wall to see if I can feel it. I wait in the downpour of water, feeling strangely nervous.

Nothing. Nothing at all.

I stifle a laugh and rub my eyes. I have to get my shit together. This is ridiculous.

I sigh and start to lay down again, shivering against the cool air, trying to creep in from the other side of the shower curtain. I adjust the curtain to try and keep the humidity in before getting into position. Just as I settle in, I notice something I hadn't before. Something so small it seemed insignificant until now.

There's a crack in the caulking of the tub, almost disguised by the build up of soap scum and mold. I put my fingers on the broken seal, and it crumbles under my touch. Bits of old silicone wash away, revealing a bigger crack. I feel the faintest chill of a breeze coming through, one that gets worse the more I mess with it. I think of what could possibly be on the other side, something other than drywall and water damage. There's no way it could be anything else. The closet is on the other side.

Against my better judgment, I decide to look in. I kneel down and take a peek, propping myself up on the ledge of the tub as I get closer and closer. I think I see something moving, and I hold my hand up to shield my face and better see through the steam.

Deep in the darkness of the cracked seal, there is nothing.

I laugh to myself again and wipe my face. Of course there's nothing. I'm just hungover, tired, and reaching. I need to sleep. I just need to sleep.

I turn the knob again to make the water hotter and lay in the shower again, feeling foolish. Just a few more minutes and I'll get out. I just need a few more minutes.

Snuggling awkwardly into the bend of my arm, I try to fall asleep again. I take a deep breath and let it out, trying to rid myself of the tension I have fabricated. There is no tapping. There never was. I focus on the spraying shower, letting it soothe me as I sink further into my own misery. I let the ambience wash over me, along with the occasional *drip-drop* from the hanging washcloth.

Drip-drop.

Drip-drop.

Drip. Drip. Drip. Drip.

I feel cool droplets hitting my temple, followed by an icy, cold draft. I shiver and turn so the water warms me, but the draft is too chilling to go away. I want to ignore it, desperately just trying to sleep and forget and be far away from my own thoughts. The drips continue, hitting my face and hair more aggressively until they're hitting my nose and eyelids. I think of the washcloth hanging, trying to rationalize the annoyance so I can just let it go.

Until something touches my hair.

There's a woman perched above, inches from my face. Her hair is long and soaked, tangled strands dangling as they drip water onto my face. I try to scream, but the air is caught in my lungs, her features petrifying me more as I have no choice but to look at her. Her eyes, mouth, and nose are missing, replaced by a collection of different sized holes. They widen and flex as she looks down at me, like a living sponge. Her naked torso is pale and abnormally long, twisting in a way that seems impossible. The rest of her is concealed by the darkness of the hole she comes from, a jagged tear where the tub surround has been peeled back to let her through. Roaches and spiders start to pour in behind her, lining the walls as I stare into the missing features of her face. She looks like she's trying to cry, a larger hole at the bottom of her face frowning like a mouth. Tiny little orbs trickle out of the holes, and I realize they are not droplets of water, but baby spiders. *Thousands* of them.

Without warning, water erupts from the holes in her face, a gushing icy blast that chokes the scream in my throat as it finally comes. I try to kick my feet but I can't move, each limb feels too heavy to lift under the weight of her presence. The water is dark and burns my eyes, and I can feel the tub filling around me. I watch her slowly fade as the water rises, blotting everything out until the last thing I see are the bugs skittering over the water's surface.

I wake to the sound of the water. I open my eyes and see the moist surroundings of the shower, and see that I'm still laying in it. No hole in the wall, no bugs, no woman; only the same crack near the ledge where I had first seen it.

I had fallen asleep.

I sit up and shiver, my limbs aching from being in such a weird position for so long. The arm I was laying on feels dead from the lack of circulation. The cascading water has lost most of its warmth, and I reach up and shut it off. It takes me a while to get to my feet, but I'm determined to get the hell out of the shower. I throw back the curtain and grab a towel, drying my face and hair before stepping out onto the bathmat. I'm shivering and ready to find clothes, but my first step out of the shower makes me freeze.

The bathmat is completely saturated, and the floor is soaked.

At first I think I left the curtain open too much, but the thought fades when I keep looking. The bathroom door is wide open, and the water continues into the hall, like I had already gotten out of the shower. Clutching the towel, I follow the trail, shivering as I leave the warmth of the bathroom behind me.

A trail of wet footprints leave the bathroom, and the air is cold as I follow them. I expect to find the woman waiting for me, but when I step into the living room, I find it empty. I only find my apartment door open, the footprints leading out.

STEP-BRO

"**S**tep-bro, can you help me?"

The words woke me from my nap like a slap to the face. I sat up in confusion, groggily wiping the sleep from my eyes as I looked around the dim room. The door to my bedroom was open, and the portentous dark of the hallway loomed in the distance. While my mind scattered to recollect what was going on, I felt for my phone in hope of clarity.

The screen was blinding. No missed calls, no texts, nothing. Only a little caution sign in the upper right corner, near the battery. *No service.*

"Hello?" I called, swinging out of bed. I was shocked I heard anything at all. I'm usually a really heavy sleeper.

The house felt empty, *abandoned* even. A feeling I was still getting used to in the new house. My mother had recently remarried after over a decade of being single. The man had money, the kind where your house echoes because there's not even furniture or bodies to fill the space. The only thing stranger than your mom shacking up with someone fifteen years older than her is house-sitting their empty home on spring break.

"Lisa?" I called once more, and got nothing but silence.

Lisa is my step-sister. Whereas I had volunteered to sit-out their ravishing vacation in exchange to catch up on Elden Ring and jerk-off in peace, Lisa had skipped to go wild while Daddy was away. Our dorms were closed for the holiday, making each other annoyed acquaintances for the week. We're both in our early twenties and single, and we don't care much for each other. I remembered laying down for a nap, in preparation of pulling an all-nighter, while Lisa waited for her ride, dressed in an outfit her father would shriek at. She said she would be back late, and it was only 9p.m..

"Hello?" My voice echoed again.

Standing in the doorway, the house was especially dark. Every light was off, the only residual glow coming from a single doorway downstairs.

The laundry room.

"Step bro? Can you help me?" a voice beckoned from downstairs, making me jump.

It was faint, but just loud enough to hear. It sounded like Lisa, but it sounded... muffled.

I sighed, already irritated.

"Lisa? What are you doing? I thought you were out!" I called, heading down the hall. I flipped every switch as I went, trying to bring in as much light as I could. The place was creepy in the dark.

"I came home to *channnge,*" she slurred, like she had been drinking, "and I got stuck."

Down the stairs, passed the framed doctorates and awards.

"Stuck in *what*?" I asked on the stairs, awaiting the reply. There was a moment of silence, like she was thinking about it.

"The wash—*washing machine.* Can you help me?" she asked, pitifully.

She had to be fucking with me.

"Are you fucking with me?" I asked, scoffing. The implication of the situation was not lost on me.

"No, I'm not. *Look,* I got sick and threw up, step-bro. Like a lot. I couldn't keep enough down. I tried to get some clothes out to change, and I got stuck, alright? Now will you help me or not? *Please?*"

I looked at the bright doorway of the laundry room, the tile stark white and pristine. Something felt wrong, like I was being set up. I thought maybe it was some kind of prank, like a TikTok trend. I considered just leaving her there; she was a bit of a brat and had been nothing but unpleasant since the recent marriage. I was just about to turn and go back to my room when she started to scream.

"STEP-BRO HELP ME OUT OF THIS FUCKING THING OR I'LL CALL THE POLICE AND MY FATHER AND THEN YOU'LL—"

"Alright! *Alright,* jeez. I'm coming, settle down, will ya? Stop calling me that," I sighed and hurried down the stairs, shuffling to the laundry room. Lisa cleared her throat like she was choking back vomit, before muttering a muffled apology.

"Thank you,"

The voice was deeper, and cracking towards the end.

"God, how much did you drink? It's still early ..." I muttered, stopping when I rounded the corner to the laundry room. The sight before me was... ridiculous.

The laundry room was so bright it was blinding, overhead fluorescents beaming above the clean floor and a matching set of machines. The dryer and washer were next to each other, with a linen cabinet on the other end. Hanging out of the expensive front-load washing machine was Lisa, only her lower half visual. It was like she had tried to climb in and fallen asleep. Not only was she *not* stuck—she wasn't moving at all.

"Lisa?" I asked, looking at her.

The room was so quiet it was unsettling. I expected vomit, a spilled purse—*something.* But it was just Lisa in the washer, her hands tucked inside like she was using them as a pillow. She was wearing the same outfit she had gone out in: a striped bodycon dress so tight you could see her panty-lines, and platform heels. One of the heels was missing, leaving a single set of painted toes laying against the tile.

"Lisa? Are you alright?" I asked from the doorway, not wanting to go in.

"Help me step-bro, I'm stuck," she said, her voice whiner than usual.

"Bullshit. You're not stuck, you're just laying in there. What is this? A joke?" I asked, looking around the room for her phone, for the setup. But there was nothing but white, no camera, no one hiding around the corner recording.

"No, *please,* I really need help, I *swear,*" Lisa started to sob, her voice breaking to the point of babbling, "help me step-bro, *please.*"

Except she wasn't moving, not even a little. It didn't even look like she was breathing. But the inside of the washing machine was dark, and I could only see the faint outline of the back of her head, her "bob" haircut tossed and completely still.

"What's... what happened?" was all I could ask. The hair stood on the back of my neck, my palms sweating. The way she was just hunched in there, not even kicking her feet, the same recited line repeated again...

"Help me step-bro."

... even as she laid face down. She looked pale—sickly, and the harder I looked, the more it looked like her face was submerged, up to her ears in what looked like...

"Help me."

Blood.

I felt like I wanted to puke. I reached in my pocket for my phone, a cold sweat beading on my forehead as I cleared my throat.

"Lisa?"

"Yes?"

"What's my name?"

I pulled out my phone and unlocked it, bringing up the keypad.

"W-what, what do you mean step-" She started, her voice started to break character.

No service.

"I wouldn't do that if I were you," Lisa's voice was deep and struggling, like she had a wet rag over her mouth. Her skinny arms reached to the mouth of the washer and started to pull herself out, and I could hear a trickling of liquid from the matted strands of her hair.

She pulled her head from the washer, and with it, a splash of deep red that washed over the tile. Her face was gone.

"Oh *god*—"

Lisa's devastated cavity of a face coughed, a sputter of blood painting the wall next to her. She reached for me with mangled hands, each digit broken in different directions. She tried to stand with her bare foot and slipped.

I left her there. I ran as fast as I could, bounding up the steps to the sounds of her trying to get up on the slippery tile. My keys were upstairs on my nightstand, if I could just get them, I'd be able t o—

A guttural moan echoed after me, an angry call that chilled my bones. The lights flickered at the sound, blinking erratically until the noise stopped.

Back down the hall, and into my bedroom. I slammed the door behind me and locked it, grabbing my keys before frantically looking for somewhere to hide. I could hear them coming, one bare foot followed by the heel. It was clumsy, but it was gaining fast.

I considered hiding under the bed, but it was too low to the ground, and I didn't know if I'd fit. I didn't want to get stuck myself—

Lisa slammed into the door, and the hinges rattled. It wasn't going to hold for long, I didn't have enough time. The closet was my only chance.

I opened the door as quietly as I could and ducked into the clothes, pulling it behind me before huddling under them in a ball.

As soon as I sat on the carpet I heard a *squelch,* like I had sat in something. As a cold, wet substance soaked into the seat of my pants, the door to my bedroom exploded.

Wood splintered inward, and I watched through the slats of the closet door as Lisa *slithered* in. She wormed her way through the hole in the door, the bleeding crater in her face reverberating angrily as her head whipped around. She flopped on the bed first, and when she couldn't find me, she slithered underneath. I watched in horror as she would temporarily pause after every movement to "sniff" the air, her head twitching as she knocked things over in my room in the process.

"Step... bro..." the monster gurgled slowly, moving impossibly as it blindly scoured the room. It twisted so far I heard ribs break, and when it propped itself up with its hands, the flesh would tear, exposing bone. Wrists cracked, knees twisted, and tendons tore.

With an angry shriek, the monster slithered out of the room. I heard it rampaging through the hall and into my mom's room, and then into Lisa's when it couldn't find me. When it had no luck, I heard it moving downstairs, and I listened to its path of destruction as it tried to find me.

When it got quiet for a while, I chanced a look with my phone to see what I was sitting in. As soon as the light went on, I had to resist the urge to scream, holding my breath and nearly pissing myself when I finally saw what was soaking into my clothes.

The carpet was caked in blood, a splotch of heavy crimson that had sprayed outward and onto my clothes. Inches away from where I sat was a single high-heeled shoe, and a bloodstained phone. *Lisa's.*

I wiped the blood from her phone and unlocked it, to see the same sickening icon of no service. I tried calling 9-1-1 with both her phone and mine, and the call wouldn't go through, even when you hit "emergency service call."

I tried to check her recent's, to see if I could find any answers to what's going on. Her call logs show several incomplete calls, five to the police, four to her father, and seven to... me. None of them were able to connect.

I checked her texts too. The last one that went through was outgoing, a response to a contact labeled only as "Him" that said:

Still picking you up? I want to get up in some guts.

To which she replied with a thumb's up emoji.

I don't know who "Him" is, but it's not the part that unsettles me the most. It's the nine failed texts that she sent to me that never made it through. While I was five feet away, sleeping.

> **Kyle, wake up**

> **My Tinder date followed me home, I'm hiding in your closet**

> **Kyle, WAKE THE FUCK UP, he's in here**

> **I don't have service**

> **I tried to wake you up**

> **I think he can hear me**

> **I don't want him to find me**

> **KYLE WAKE THE FUCK UP**

> **KYLE**

I've been in here for a while now, and the phone's about to die. I don't know what it is, but it's still down there. I would've tried to sneak past it, but it hears everything, I even had to mute my keyboard on my phone so I could type this out. I tried calling my mom, the police, my step-dad. Nothing will go through. It just says I don't have signal.

I thought of jumping out the window, but I think it'll get me before I can get out. It's gotten faster, the more of Lisa it leaves behind. Last I heard, it was moving things around and stacking them, like it's trying to keep me from getting out. I'm going to try and post this somewhere, and see if I can get enough signal for it to go through. If you get this, please send help. And if you get in here, *do not* help her out of the washing machine.

Lisa, I'm sorry.

Think I might try the window after all.

TURNAROUND

It happens all the time, and I can't help but find it irritating. I live on the outskirts of town, less than a mile from a busy highway, and people pull into my driveway at all hours of the day. It always makes me nervous, wondering if someone is dropping by unannounced. Only to see them sit at the end for a moment, before reversing out and driving away.

It's most unsettling at night. Seeing the headlights cut through the trees in my front yard while they sit there. It makes me wonder if someone's scoping my house out, like they're thinking of robbing me. I park my car in the garage, so it always looks like I'm not home. In the end, they always drive away, and I'm left feeling foolish at someone's lack of direction.

A few days ago, however, someone pulled in and didn't leave.

I stood and watched them from the window of my living room, peeking out through the blinds. The car sat there suspiciously, idling just at the end of the driveway. I thought maybe they were lost and checking the GPS on their phone, trying to figure out where they missed a turn. I try not to be a total jerk about it, and give them time to figure out where they're going before jumping to conclusions. But it was after eleven o'clock at night, and not only were they interrupting my movie, they were weirding me out.

When the car stayed there for five minutes, I started to get worried. I raised the blinds and started waving, to see if I could get some kind of reaction. The car continued to idle there, the faint trail of exhaust rising in the chilly night. Nobody turned on the dome light, nobody got out. Nothing. I just stood there watching, wondering if I should go out there, or call the police. Dialing 911 seemed a little ridiculous without even going out and seeing first, so I did something I *really* didn't want to.

I went to see why they were sitting there.

I put on my shoes and pulled on a jacket. I brought my phone for light or in case I needed to help them call a tow truck or something. I thought the best case scenario was maybe they got a flat tire, and their phone had died and they were too nervous to knock on the door. Like I said, it was after eleven, and knocking on someone's door at that hour could be just as shady as watching them sit at the end of my driveway.

Against my better judgment, I stepped outside. I could hear the engine running in the distance, along with a chorus of crickets chirping in the night. It took me a few seconds to get the courage to walk out there; the driveway is pretty long, and it's really dark. Everything feels scarier in the middle of the night, especially with no neighbors close by.

I swallowed hard and started walking, keeping my eyes on the car as I walked over. I turned on the flashlight function on my phone and tried to keep a steady pace on the way. Gravel crunched under my feet, and my palms started to sweat. Maybe they were drunk and fell asleep. Maybe it was a couple of young kids lost on a late night out.

When I got about twenty feet away, I got a sick feeling in my stomach. Something felt off, especially when I could see the driver behind the wheel. They were just looking at me, like they were frozen. I could only faintly make out their eyes, a pale visage within the darkness of the front seat.

"Hello?" I asked aloud, trying not to sound as nervous as I was.

No response. The driver didn't even blink.

I took a couple steps closer, trying to see if there was anyone else in there with them. The urge to call the police itched at me more the closer I got.

"You lost? This is private property," I called out again, the features in the driver's face looking more unsettling the closer I got. I could only see their eyes, their nose. Why couldn't I see anything else? Why weren't they moving?

The headlights were blinding, making it hard to see. I kept pushing forward, holding up a hand to try and block so I could see. I had no choice but to get closer, and try to get around to the driver's side to get a better look.

More crunching footsteps, and their car getting louder. The driver didn't move a muscle, didn't motion to me or anything. I realized I was holding my breath, the anxiety welling within me as I approached. The driver looked like a woman, her hands in front of her, holding the wheel. But it was so dark in there, I couldn't *see* her hands, only the unmoving stare.

A strong feeling of foreboding radiated from the eerie car, and my body begged to turn and run back to the house. Something was wrong. Very, *very,* wrong.

I walked around the front of the vehicle to the driver's side, and held up my flashlight to see them. They didn't turn to look at me; they didn't do anything. My eyes slowly calibrated what was in front of me, and when it finally pieced together, I wanted to scream.

The woman was dead, her lifeless eyes frozen on my house, unable to look away. Her throat had been slashed, and the entire car was spattered with blood. Duct tape was everywhere; a single wrap across her forehead to hold her in place, a strip over her mouth so she couldn't speak, and several tight binds around her wrists to keep them to the steering wheel.

Her hands had been removed.

I called the police, frantically looking everywhere as the world seemed to be caving in on me. An operator picked up immediately, and through my terrified ramble, I subconsciously took in the scene as I explained what was happening.

There was nobody in the backseat, and no signs of anyone leaving. I started to panic more, looking in the trees, and back towards the house, expecting to see someone watching. But there was nobody else, nobody except me and the butchered woman.

The operator instructed me to go back inside and lock the doors until help arrived. I sprinted back to the front door, the sounds of my own footsteps haunting me as I made my way back to the porch. Once inside, I slammed the door and locked it, flinching at every sound as the voice on the other line tried to keep me quiet. My heart raced so hard in my chest I thought I would have a heart attack.

The police arrived in less than two minutes. One car at first, with an officer getting out of the vehicle gun-drawn. Then another. Then two more. The fire department was next, and the wailing siren bled into the barrage of lights that lit up my entire house. It didn't feel safe to be there, even after officers came in and searched the house, and scoured the entire property.

They didn't find anyone, and the killer didn't leave anything behind.

The days that followed blurred together. I had to take some time off work, between the questioning and my driveway turning into a crime scene, I couldn't go anywhere if I tried. I didn't sleep much, between the police, a lawyer, and the news crews, I wasn't alone for a while. They searched everything; the basement, the attic, the woods behind my house. They even looked in the crawlspace to see if they were holed up in there. There was no evidence left behind, no inclination of where they went, either.

The killer was never found.

I didn't learn much about the woman I found, other than that they suspect she was picked at random on her way home from work.

Eventually, things went back to normal, and I was allowed to go back to work. It was a relief to get out of the house; even after they towed that poor woman's car away, I couldn't help but think of it every time I looked outside. Getting into town and back behind my desk was a welcome distraction, and once I was able to busy my mind it was easier to pretend it was all just a bad dream.

That was, until I was driving home last night. I was about halfway home when I started noticing an *odor*, like I had driven past some roadkill. I tried rolling up the windows and it got worse, a heavy, rotting smell that made me gag.

I realized it was something *inside the car*.

When I pulled over to find it, I looked under the seats and in the trunk, thinking maybe I had left out some raw meat from the last time I went shopping. I didn't find anything, and I found myself scratching my head at a loss.

Until I looked at the glovebox, and saw it was leaking.

When I hit the button and opened it, the scent exploded into the cab, along with a cloud of buzzing flies.

Stuffed inside the glove box was the pair of women's hands, decomposed and swelling against the duct tape that wrapped around them.

A LATE GOODBYE

The wall of sand was intimidating before me.

I put my car in park and returned my hands to the wheel, my gut twisting at the thought of getting out. The sands of Mount Baldy had changed drastically since the last time I had been there. The notorious hill was roped off and denied human entrance, with markers directing a new path to the beach on the other side. The bittersweet memory that played in my head didn't match what lay before me, and I couldn't help but take it as a sign.

Just get this done, and get on your way. Last band-aid.

My mental coaching didn't make me feel any less sick to my stomach. I looked in the backseat at the neat stack of luggage as I tried to pull myself together. A new life, packed into three suitcases. I was so close now. This was my last stop before the airport.

Why did it have to be the hardest one?

I looked back at the sand, the steep wall so smooth it looked like glass. The bittersweet memory returned, long-lost echoes of a nice kiss and laughter playing over in my head like a recording, the whisper of a perfect moment in time fading before I felt the hooks of the pain that followed. I shut it out, holding on to the hope that when I pulled away from here, the memory would get buried in the sand.

I grabbed my phone from the passenger seat and unlocked it. The screen filled with my reason for being here, the text that baited me probably just as well as it intended to; a message from my ex-boyfriend, Brendan.

> **Heard you're leaving town. Can I at least say goodbye? I'll be at our old spot until dusk.**

I threw open the door and stepped out, not wanting to delay a second longer. The air felt humid in the enclosed parking lot, the border of forestation trapping the air like a little capsule. I followed the markers to the newly constructed detour, and found the entrance to the trail started with a wooden staircase into the foliage. I swallowed hard and crossed the lot.

By the time I made it to the landing, a couple was heading down. Sunglasses and faces reddened by the sun, equally cheery and exhausted from a day at the beach. They nodded as we passed each other, and our pleasantries were automatic.

"Nice day for it, enjoy."

"Let's hope so."

The miniature boardwalk gave way to a beaten path of loose sand, leaves, and slag. It didn't stand up to the upward beauty of the old dunes, and the man-made trail came with its own sense of foreboding. The trail dipped with the slope of the hill only to grow steeper the closer you got to the beach. I was thankful for my shoes, but knew the sand would work its way in anyway. The thought of the little grains scrunching between my toes on my flight made me agitated. Maybe after I dealt with this, I wouldn't care so much. I tried to enjoy the beauty of the lakeside wilderness, but my mind kept pulling away, to the rollercoaster that had been mine and Brendan's relationship.

Brendan and I met in college. He was handsome, flirty, and had a love for partying. I fell for him immediately, his dorky smoothness feeling like a breath of fresh air in the monotony of courses that my life had become.

In the beginning, it was normal. *Nice.* Awkward hangouts playing video games together, and flirting after Burger King. It was the first time I really came out of my shell; I wasn't big on the party scene, but wasn't opposed to trying new things. When things got a little more serious and we started sleeping together, I exchanged lonely nights and Netflix with staying over and a bottle of wine. It felt good to let a little loose, as I had spent most of my teenage years studying hard and staying in when everyone else was out having fun.

On the days we didn't spend together, he would be off with his friends, or staying up getting high. In the beginning I didn't mind. We were younger, and life is meant for experimenting and having fun. And when it was just the two of us, he was sweet, and he made our time special.

When I got out of my comfort zone enough, we met at Mount Baldy, sharing a joint and watching the clouds as the day passed by. We would always sit on a little cliff spot, an overgrown portion of dune that overlooked the shore a few dozen feet above.

We dated for quite a while before things changed. He would show up to classes late, or miss them completely. His part-time job would never pan out, and in time I would pay for his food, and sometimes weed and beer. I didn't mind, really. I was totally in love with him, and assumed it was just part of his "broke-college phase", one that would change in time.

But it never did. The jobs never lasted, and the money never saved. I laughed with him through the highs and stood by him through the lows, watching him drink or smoke away each little paycheck until he was broke and depressed, often trying to sweet-talk me to "help him out one last time". In the beginning I caved, *a lot.* Sometimes it was "just a pint so I can stay up with the boys", others it was "just enough weed to get me through the weekend".

I arrived at a peak in the hill, one accompanied by colorful hazard signs featuring stick figures in peril. I stopped to look, taking a moment to catch my breath a little. The climb was pretty steep to this point, so it was a pleasant distraction. Bold letters warning of the unstable sand in the roped off area, as well as the threat of riptide when swimming in the lake below.

As I continued down the trail, so did my thoughts of Brendan. The longer I went, the more it started to hurt, each step digging up the past in the wake of my new future. It wasn't *always* bad, but when every smiling moment was stained with the ugliness of another, it was hard to discern if there was any real happiness in the relationship. As much as I wanted to turn heel and leave, I felt like it was necessary to close this chapter so I could grow, and hopefully one day flourish from it. Even if the late goodbye was too-little too-late.

By the time I had started the uphill again, my mind wandered into a carousel of emotion, the good and the bad brought up hand in hand, each a much different moment in time:

A passionate hook-up in the backseat at the campus, to the pregnancy scare when he was too drunk to pull out. Staying up late watching movies together, replaced by him falling asleep within the first five minutes because he was too stoned. Recalling a special time when he cooked me dinner, fading away to him sending me out for fast food late at night because it wasn't safe for him to drive.

The trail angled upward, and as my legs continued on autopilot, so did the memories.

The sweet purchase of a promise ring, only to see him looking through my purse when he thought I was sleeping. Long walks and held hands through town, then bailing him out for public intoxication. The first I love yous, buried under the sound of a belligerent argument. The memory of sharing a joint at Mount Baldy, only to recall when I revisit here alone to cry. Spending graduation alone, weeks after he dropped out. A promise of how things would get better, only to be forgotten.

I was pulled from my recollections to see a fork in the road, and with it, an old wooden sign. Two arrows pointing in opposite directions, each with an old painted label. The sign on the left read "SHORE", and on the right, "PEAK". My guess was I would find Brendan on the right in our old spot, if there was anything left of it from the erosion. I took a deep breath and headed that direction, into a tight corridor of trees that led to the peak.

I hoped he'd be well. I was worried he wasn't. Ducking into the trees, I realized I wasn't prepared for either.

I could feel the breeze from the lake now. Orange and violet rays poked through the trees, accompanied by the faint sound of waves crashing in the distance. The path was tighter, and it was dark, the uneven ground within the trees making me anxious. Several long-dried layers of leaves and the remnants of fallen rotten trees made me feel like I didn't belong, but not as much as the light at the end of the tunnel. The urge to turn and leave was overwhelming, and I felt the preemptive knot forming in my stomach. I tried to relax and breathe, and assure myself it would be alright. By the time I made it to the peak, I realized I hadn't been breathing at all.

Brendan was waiting at the cliff, sitting on the edge quietly as he watched the water below. He seemed to sense my arrival, looking in my direction just as I emerged from the trees. His face lit up for a moment, a split second of hope before the reminder of why I had come out. His eyes were hollow, his face slack. A glimmer of a smile tried to shine through, but I could tell it was forced.

"Brendan," I said, and he got up from the ledge. Sand crumbled away and trickled down to the shore below.

"Faye. You made it," he said quietly, brushing himself off. He looked nervous, and looked around awkwardly as he approached.

"Yeah," I said, looking solemnly at the water. I followed its smooth rhythm from the horizon to the shore, watching it get choppier as it reached the sand. It was a beautiful view and would've been a nice evening if it were any other day. He approached and looked like he was going to offer a hug, and decided against it.

"Thanks for coming," he said, fidgeting a little before gesturing to me. "You look good."

I felt a tinge of sadness as I looked at him; baggy clothes, torn shoes, his hair and face untrimmed. The same as he looked when I left, although he had lost some weight.

You look tired—

"You look good, too. How have you been? How are things?" I said, wishing I had something better to say.

He shrugged, fidgeting again. He looked at the water nervously, before looking at his feet.

"Same old, you know. One day at a time," he paused to nudge the sand with his shoe, before adding, "not as good as you though, I bet."

My eyes wanted to well up, but I pushed it off.

"Is that how you wanted to do this? Make this *my* fault?" I asked plainly, standing my ground.

"N-no—no. It's not what you think. *Look.* I just wanted to say I'm sorry, is all. That's it. I'm sorry," Brendan put his hands up in defense, something I had seen him do a hundred times. It felt like it was different this time, but it always felt like that. His eyes were puffy, like he had been crying. There was something off about his demeanor. He looked rushed—agitated.

A cool breeze blew from the lake, and the waves tossed on the shore below. I focused on it and took a deep breath, trying to shrug off the emotion rising within. Brendan fidgeted more, his eyes settling on the ground.

"What's going on, Brendan?" I asked, rubbing my temples. I could feel a faint ringing in my ears, what I assumed was the start of a tension headache.

"Nothing. It's just—I heard you were leaving. I've been thinking about you a lot, and all the good times we've had. Things I'll miss when you're gone. I just wanted to tell you... I'm sorry. For everything. I know I haven't been good to you, and you have every right to move on. I get that. It just hurts, you know? Knowing you'll be gone," Brendan sniffled, fighting back another round of tears.

I sighed. The words were familiar, a rehash of a plea from the past. We had been here before, but no matter how the presentation went, the outcome was the same.

"Brendan—"

"I can't live without you."

His statement hung in the air, the dead weight of them blocking out the sounds of the lake. I tried to look into his eyes, but he seemed unable to look at me.

"That's what this was about? One last attempt to keep me in? *I'm done*, Brendan. You know that. Is that why you called me out here? I'm leaving the *country.*"

"I know—" he protested.

"I have a flight in an hour. I can't—you think I'd just drop everything and give you one more chance? After all this time?"

"No."

"Then why am I here?"

"I just," Brendan sighed, looking at the lake once more, "I just wanted to talk, that's all. I just wanted to say goodbye."

"Have you been drinking?" I blurted, before I could stop myself. Brendan took it like a silent slap, a single tear running down his cheek.

"No. *No.* I'm clear. I've never been this clear."

I didn't know what to say. The water started getting choppier, the waves slapping into the shore more aggressively. There were no words I could say to make this better, no way to smooth it over. After a moment of silence, Brendan shuffled over to the spot he was sitting and sat back down.

I looked at the corridor of trees—my exit. Brendan started to cry, holding his face in his hands. The sound still wounded me. I checked the time on my phone. I still had a little bit. I sighed and sat next to him. After a while, he spoke again.

"You remember when we used to sit out here? Just us, watching the waves?" he said quietly.

The memory of us smoking together, and me bawling alone.

"Yeah."

Brendan sniffled and wiped his eyes, and together we watched the lake. I watched the slow rear back of the next wave, and listened to the collective *woosh* as it prepared to hit the shore. Underneath the peace of it all, it felt *angry.*

He said nothing for a time, collecting himself. I could tell he wanted to say more, so I waited.

"There's been this pain inside me. For a long time, now. I don't know how to get rid of it. It didn't start when you left—i-it's been there. And I've been trying to ignore it. Trying to dull it. Nothing seems to work. Ever since you left... I just can't take it anymore. It's too much. Gnawing at me, every day."

As I listened, my eyes drifted to the lake, a strange pale shape drawing me in. It poked through the water, a slow bulbous birth that rose unnaturally through the water's surface. The ringing noise was starting to get stronger, like it was echoing over the waves.

"Brendan—"

"I can't do it. Everything in the world, the weight of it all. I don't have it in me. I'm just tired—too tired. The weight is too heavy, and I don't think I can do it without you."

"What are you saying?" I asked, half looking at him, half looking at the water. The more I looked at the shape, the more it looked like *a face.*

"Were you ever happy? With me?" he said, and I looked at him. His lip was quivering, tears streaming down both cheeks. I reached out and touched his shoulder, and it only made it worse.

"You know I was happy. For a lot of it, but you couldn't—*I couldn't—*"

In the distance, the shape continued to rise. The pale, scarred face of a head gave way to a neck, and with it, shoulders.

"Do you see that? Is there someone—"

Brendan looked at it and paid it no mind, like it wasn't there.

"The pain *has to end.* I can't take it. Especially if you're not with me. I'll sink. I can't do it. Buried under the weight of it all. The pain is too much."

Through the water, a torso followed the head. Bloated and white, the skin and muscle tattered. Like it had been beaten by the waves for a long time. The face looked up at us, eyes like two black pearls, most of its lips missing around its mouth. Its jaw a tight clamp of exposed teeth.

"Brendan, what is that? Do you see it?" I asked, and he ignored me.

Whatever it was, it was almost out of the water. A torso covered in pulpy gashes and little bites, saturated strands of flesh dangling from every light-colored wound. Once its shriveled nudity rose from the water, I shook Brendan.

"Brendan, what the fuck—"

"Aren't you tired, Faye?"

He looked into my eyes, his glazed and defeated stare burrowing deep. He didn't even look at it, but I knew he knew.

The wind picked up, an icy gust that shivered my bones. I can't explain it, but it felt... *wrong.* Brendan refused to look away from me, even as dripping toes hovered over the water. The pieces in my mind didn't make sense, but the look in his eyes told me it was his doing.

"Brendan, *what have you done?*"

He blinked away the accusation, tears trickling. Another crashing wave, louder than the last.

"I found something to take it away," was all he said, before lightly shaking his head.

"W-what—how? What did you do?" I asked, watching the swollen being drift closer. There was an inaudible malice to it, the way its lifeless gaze peered up at us from the lake, with every gaining inch. There was an unnatural static to its float, and the water's surface rippled beneath it.

Brendan finally looked at it, a sickening acceptance in his eyes. Thoughts of our past raced through my head, and through the frantic catalog, I wondered how it all went horribly wrong. I was there for him. I *tried.* Thoughts of shared smiles, dreamy eyes, and laughs raced through my head, but the primal urge to flee pushed itself to the front.

"We should go. We have to go, *now,*" I urged, but he didn't listen.

"It should only hurt for a moment," he said, and looked out at the lake. The monster was close enough I could see the wispy remains on its scalp.

I couldn't watch him die. Not like this.

"You don't have to do this—we can run. Let me help you," I pleaded.

Brendan just sat there, the wind tossing his shaggy hair. To my surprise, he started to smile. He leaned against me, and even though his whisper was soft, it cut right through me.

"I told him he could have us *both.*"

I looked at him, and he started to laugh. A maniacal, unhinged cackle that echoed over the beach. The monster over the water was getting closer, its feet dangling over the sand as it drifted in. I looked into its abyssal eyes, and the ringing in my ears started to blare. Brendan's text message played through my head over and over.

Can I at least say goodbye?

I got up from the ledge and ran, Brendan's laughter echoing even as I disappeared into the trees. I ran as fast as the sand would let me. Panic settled in as the sand bogged down my footing. Each hurried stride kicked dust in all directions.

I passed the sign for the fork in the road and quickly descended the downhill portion of the trail. The air was cold now, chilling the sweat on my forehead as I reached the dip and proceeded to climb.

My legs burned as I went as fast as I could, huffing through every clumsy step.

The pain has to end.

Especially if I'm not with you.

Brendan's words taunted me as I ran, every footfall haunted by his laughter and the harrowing floating corpse.

Aren't you tired, Faye?

By the time I made it to the bold warning signs, the sounds of the waves had faded. I took a moment to catch my breath, my lungs burning from the rapid hike. There was no wind in the trees, and no breeze from the lake. Only the stagnant humidity of the forest. I looked to see if there was anyone on the trail or the parking lot below, but there was nobody in sight. The sun was setting, and a dimness was falling quickly.

Off in the distance, I heard a blood-curdling scream. It sounded like Brendan, but the longer it went, the higher it got. It was like his voice was being ripped apart.

Then it was gone.

I turned heel and ran, pushing down the wooden staircase I had climbed not long ago. I jogged across the parking lot to my car, already fumbling the keys from my pocket.

I unlocked the door, shoved the key in the ignition, and started the car.

Ahead of me was the wall of sand. It was so flat and pristine, and the clarity of it made me wonder if any of this was even real. Maybe I had just made it up in a panic—an excuse to break away from Brendan. Maybe my guilt or selfishness had gotten the better of me, and I pretended it was there so I had an out. Maybe I just had a panic attack.

Ahead, the sand starts to tremble. The little granules vibrating and skittering, like the dunes themselves are scared. The center of the wall starts to shift, and with a deafening blast of sound, a balding head pushes through. Two unblinking black eyes, staring at me.

I threw it in reverse and backed out of my spot, wincing against the ringing as the monster forced its way toward me. The tires squealed as I left the dunes behind me, merging back onto the road wildly with my foot pushing the pedal to the floor.

I stayed on the road for a while, cutting back through town until I hit the highway. I drove straight to the airport, focusing only on the speedometer and the occasional check in the rear-view mirror. There was nothing behind me except slower cars and shrinking roads as I left the nightmare behind me.

I pushed away thoughts of it as I arrived at the hectic roundabout of the airport, monotonously pulling in and surrendering my car to a valet. I got my luggage from the backseat and proceeded through TSA, and numbly checked in for my flight.

Each time I looked out the windows of the terminal, I saw nothing but the congested traffic of the vehicles outside, and the corralled populace within.

It wasn't real. It couldn't be. There's no feasible way. Brendan was just crazy. It must've been stress. I just blew it out of proportion—saw what I *wanted* to see.

Boarding the plane, I left the past behind. No more guilt, no more pain. As we broke through the clouds, I settled into my seat and thought of a better future.

I arrived at the hotel in the middle of the night. The streets were dark and empty, but I embraced the unknown environment and let it wash my old life away. I have a busy day tomorrow. There's so much to do on the road ahead, but for now, I'm too tired to think about it.

The sheets are soft, and the bed is comfortable. I turned on the TV for some white noise.

I hope it'll help with the ringing in my ears.

THE BREAKROOM TABLE

I only had fifteen minutes to go when the intercom chimed overhead, the distraught and obviously frustrated voice echoed across long dusty aisles.

"All employees report to the supervisor's office. *Now.*"

The final tone made me uneasy, like I was getting sent to the principal's office. I checked the time on my phone. So preciously close to leaving, and now this. I wheeled my cart over to the nearest rack and started walking in the direction of the supervisor's office, in the center of the plant.

I work at an assembly factory. Portable and industrial compressors. I'm a "material handler" as they call the position, which is a fancy way of saying scramble around to find parts that aren't where they're supposed to be, and chase down where they actually are to deliver them to their proper spot. A repeating cycle of hell, honestly. Except with air compressors.

"Ayyyy girl, aren't you supposed to be gone by now?" I heard the unmistakable voice of Hot Tuna, and heard him jogging up behind me.

We call him Hot Tuna because he's always microwaving tuna and broccoli on lunch.

"Hey HT. Yeah, less than fifteen minutes," I said, as he matched my pace. He was a big guy, huge into weights and carb-cutting. He ran the test cell on the shift, mostly machines that were backlogged due to leaks or faulty wiring. Although he must've been hiding somewhere on his phone away from the cameras, because he clearly wasn't in his work area.

"Always something stupid with this place, I swear," he said as we came to an intersection in the racks and turned left.

We were a skeleton crew on night shift, a slow expansion due to the company's recent boom in business. Something about a partner company blowing up, blah blah. There were four of us in total on the shift—three grunts and a supervisor.

"Sounds like somebody fucked up, bad," HT said, his phone going off. He dug it out and started clicking away at a text, nearly bumping into a palette jutting out from the second shelf. The place was a mess.

"Yeah, just a shame I couldn't escape first," I groaned, wishing I was on my way to the time clock. I was thinking of my date night, and the four hours of PTO I put in to be able to make it. Of course, of all days for an "emergency" meeting.

"He must've been hawking the cameras again, maybe it was—" HT was cut off by what sounded like a dog barking through the vocal cords of a human. Part Timer.

We call him Part Timer because he calls off work once a week, almost every week. He works in assembly and is probably on his way out.

"What did you fuckers do now? I'm sure it's something I didn't do," PT joked, making another grotesque dog noise before addressing us, "wattup HT. Big Water."

They call me Big Water because I always have a giant water bottle. It's a 1.75 liter. I cut caffeine two weeks ago, and have been drowning my sorrows in H20 since. It's not really helping. I'm miserable. My name is the only one that doesn't get abbreviated, nobody knows why, but it's funny.

"Part Time. What did you do now?" HT clapped him on the shoulder, the way a bear would bully a small child.

"Hey, I made it in today. At least," PT coughed as we weaved through a line of unfinished machines, large portables with their guts exposed. He chuckled shamefully, and we laughed.

"Let's hurry up and get this done so Big Water can get out of here. She's got PTO," HT said, motioning for the door.

"You're leaving early? When?" he gasped, scowling.

"Seven," I grinned.

"Oh, fuck you," PT rolled his eyes.

"At least I earned the time," I shrugged.

"Fair."

Beyond the machines was a little dusty shanty, an "office" erected in the middle of two different assembly lines. Seeing it made me feel nervous. There was no shortage of the usual antics in the shop, but the tone on the intercom. Somebody fucked up. Pretty bad from the sounds of it.

The little shanty felt oppressive as we drew near, and I could feel the atmospheric oppression of someone higher on the totem pole. It was a uniquely dangerous vibe, especially for a non-union shop.

"All right. Let's see what Piss Baby wants, and get you on your way," HT chuckled, reaching for the door.

We call him Piss Baby, because he's the supervisor.

HT opened the door and held it for us, probably so he could tower innocently behind us. As the three of us filed in, I felt like I was back in high-school, awaiting a broad scolding because someone placed a tactful whoopie-cushion, or wouldn't stop handing gum out in class. It felt simultaneously sweaty and trivial.

PB sat at one of the three desks in the little "office", obviously furious, and sweating. His eyes reflected the plethora of cameras from his screen, his eyeballs flicking from one to another, like he'd catch something as we walked in. HT was the first to pipe up.

"Hey boss, what's up—" the cutoff was swift and angry.

"All I can say is: *Are you fucking kidding me?* I like to think I run a *pretty loose* leash—I'm cool with most of the shit I have to put up with—but *this?* I don't even know where to begin. I don't even know—who in their right mind? To pull this shit. The blatant disrespect, I-I can't even believe it. The atrocity, to do something like this. Why? *Why?* If I find out *who*, you'll be on the unemployment line faster than, faster than—as if the vandalism in the fences, and the ripped-up roadkill wasn't enough. You had to do this? Who did it?" he turned to us, out of breath, flustered.

A coyote, or something like it, had been burrowing under the fence that surrounded the property. It seemed to be happening at night, when there were way less people around. Not to mention the roadkill carcasses left around company grounds, that seemed like they had been... *played with* before leaving them as a present.

"What's going on here?" I asked, trying to be a voice of reason. PB scoffed and started clicking with his mouse, focusing and enlarging one specific camera angle, then zooming in, all on a live feed of footage.

"He's good with the cameras, that's why they hired him," PT muttered under his breath.

"This. This! Does anyone want to explain themselves? Anyone want to 'shine a light' on this depravity?" PB was irate, pointing to the screen that we all started to home in on.

The little flatscreen showed the layout of the breakroom through the window of a camera stationed above one of the lines, zoomed in on a specific table top.

On top of the table was a pile of what could only be described as... shit.

PB continued, spittle flying from everything syllable.

"I go to get some coffee—just some coffee, and what do I find? Shit. I found that someone, one of our employees, has *shit* on the table. A human being. On a place people eat, for god's sake. Why?!" he leaned back in his chair, exhausted.

We all looked at each other, then without a word, HT leaned in and eyed it seriously.

"Hmm. Yeah, that's definitely not me. If it was me, it would've been bigger. Much bigger, probably."

"This isn't a fucking joke. I had half a mind to call corporate tonight. Just imagine how that would turn out. We'd all be fired," PB fumed.

"Wait, you don't think one of us *actually* did that, do you?" I asked, unable to look away from the mess through the camera's feed on the monitor. The more I looked at it, the nastier it got. Clearly someone was having a hard time properly digesting.

"Surely there has to be... uh... some kind of explanation," PT said, scratching his head, a stupid smile on his face. I wondered for a moment if it *was* him, but the more I looked at the pile, the less it looked human. It almost looked like there were bones in it.

"This isn't funny," PB warned. HT shrugged. The three of us looked at each other, probably conjuring the mental image of someone going through the trouble to squat on the table.

"Look, I have PTO that starts in like, less than ten minutes. Can you just cut to the chase and tell us who did it? I'm sure you looked at the cameras."

"That's the problem. Whoever did it toyed with the footage. It gets all distorted. Someone fucked with it. I don't know which one of you did it—maybe it's all of you," he looked at us one by one, his face flustered. It looked like smoke would billow from his ears at any moment.

"Well that's obvious. A ghost did it," PT said, chewing his lip. Right before he burst into laughter. HT only lasted two seconds before he joined in. Funny as it was, I couldn't help but look at the clock. *Eight minutes.* I still had to wash my hands and walk to the time clock.

"I should fire you both," PB seethed.

"If you fire them both, you'll be stuck cleaning it up. I'm out of here for the night." I tapped my wrist where a watch would've been, had I worn one.

PB groaned. I made my way to the door of the little shanty.

"*Look.* I don't have any evidence either of you did this, *but I know one of you did.* I don't know how you pulled it off, but you did. Ha-ha. All I ask is you guys get this shit cleaned up in time for day-"

HT and PT chuckled, and PB stood from his desk, momentarily halting the amusement.

"I'm serious. Get this—*mess*, cleaned up. And since she's leaving, it's up to you two. If you clean it up, I'll let it slide. But. If I somehow find *how* one of you did this, I'm firing the hell out of you. Even you, Janice."

I felt myself freeze at the door, my hand hanging just inches from the knob. PT coughed and cleared his throat.

"Uh, her name is Big Water,"

It took everything in me not to snort.

"Clean the mess up. Now," The supervisor seemed at his breaking point, and I could hear the other two filing out behind me.

Hot Tuna and Part Timer followed me out of the supervisor's office, barely containing themselves. By the time we weaved back into the part racks they burst into laughter, a depraved cackling that echoed for rows of dusty stock. Something Piss Baby surely heard.

"Oh my god. That's good, that's so good," PT wheezed.

"Dude, my fucking sides. His face—please tell me you saw his face! Man. Don't even care if I get fired," HT said.

"Does that mean *you* shit the table?" I asked.

More deranged laughter, the I-wanna-go-home-and-not-be-here-kind.

"Like I said, it would be bigger," HT shrugged.

"I don't even think with my wonderful diet of alcohol and pills I could produce whatever was on that table. He's either fucking with us, or it was you," PT said, before stopping and looking at me.

HT stopped as well, suppressing what looked like another booming laugh.

"*Stop.* The only thing I had backed up in me was the urge to get the fuck out of here." They looked at each other, and promptly died.

Jokes aside, we made our way to the locker rooms, and sadly for the other two, the janitorial closet. Neither of us really addressed who was behind the monstrous "shit" in the breakroom, nor did we seem to want to talk about it. It was apparent HT and PT were going to clean it, but there was an unsaid disturbance underneath all of it; whether someone didn't want to mop someone else's shit or their own, or simply just questioning how a shitty job had gotten them this far. Or why they'd compliantly clean it.

Hot Tuna had a baby on the way, and was currently trying to soak up whatever overtime he could get outside the skeleton shift.

Part Timer had mentioned in passing that he had trouble holding a job for long, and was trying to make right by his girlfriend to fend off some of his building debt.

We parted ways, and selfishly I ducked into the women's locker room, ready to get changed and out of there for the night. I changed quickly, feeling the agonizing fly of time at work against my precious minutes outside of it. Despite the laughs of the current "vandalization" on the company property, there was something unsettling about the whole ordeal.

Someone shitting on the table was funny. But the fact that nobody knew what was going on, or at least pretended not to, was equally fucked up. I chalked it up to laughs being laughs, but as I left the women's locker room, I couldn't help but feel sick at the thought of it.

My last memory of Hot Tuna and Part Timer was watching them wheel the mop bucket reluctantly towards the break room as

I passed them to the time clock. They snickered and sneered as I left in good fun, but when I got a chance to *actually see* the sight for myself, it carried the weight of a punch to the stomach.

The closest table to the door of the break room had been absolutely covered in what could only be described as 'shit', but that was almost putting it lightly. There was something more to the collected mass on the table—something sinister lurking within the waste. In my brief time passing the view of the collected rectal purge, I couldn't help but notice the signs of jagged bone jutting through the waste. Or the sickly runoff of blood that secreted through the pile.

"Take it easy, Big Water," HT said.

"Yeah, have one for us," PT added.

I returned the courtesy and said that I would and that they should too, but as I swiped my timecard and hurried across the parking lot, I couldn't help but forget about the event altogether.

Work seems grueling and important while you're present, but once you left the premises—or more importantly, get to your car—the world you leave behind ceases to exist. I don't mean that heartlessly. It's the same for me as it is for everyone else.

So I hurried home. Showered and changed into something nice, and applied makeup while thinking of a good glass of wine and the hours of monotonous labor I would luckily be missing out on. The hours you wished more than anything you could skip, despite how fun the banter was.

I was at dinner when the texts started to come in. I glanced at the first one, barely registering the words before locking my phone. The waiter was approaching with the food, and I wanted to place myself as far away from the working life as I could. Even as the table was set with a nice, seared steak and fingerling potatoes, I couldn't help but think of the text as it played through my mind.

The text was from Hot Tuna, but I canceled it out just the same. Readying my knife and fork, I assumed he had decided to leave after having to clean up the unexplainable mess. I didn't blame him, but I was surprised HT went through the effort to text me. It was something that happened quite regularly, aside from the nights where there was a discovered shit in the break room.

I put my phone on silent, and continued the night like any other.

The wine was starting to get to me, and I began to forget about my phone, as well as anything else that faded outside of my night out. The phone continued to vibrate, and I continued to ignore it, deciding whatever it was it could wait until morning. By the time I was on my third glass, I forgot I had a phone entirely, until my SO reminded me I left it on the table as we were about to leave.

The rest of my night moved in a smooth and sultry blur, now that I was far away from the chained anxiety of finishing a shift and watching the clock.

When I awoke, I saw the building on fire.

Not in person, but on the news. The erratic and inexperienced sprawl of a local news team handling a camera while the fire department put it out, my hungover brain trying to make sense of the heavy spray of a hose that blasted the plant from a safe distance. My mind jumbled half-forgotten memories of the night before, and while I watched the local news report, I couldn't help but feel for my phone.

I had several missed calls, as well as a number of text messages.

The first was from Hot Tuna, one I vaguely recall seeing a glimpse of.

His other messages were rushed—fucked up compared to what he usually texted.

> Theres no one here, someone shut the lights off, I'm trying to find PB. You guys organize this?

I felt a sickening feeling in my gut, seeing that as his last message. The next string of notifications being from PT.

> Fuck you for leaving early, drink a bottle of wine for me

> Whoever made this shit ate roadkill and eggs, are you sure it wasn't you

> Gonna need to shower after we mopped that, it was D-Day up in there

> Tuna is missing. Someone shut off the lights, and I'm lurking on the portable line. This place is a dump

> Seriously, no fire department or anything, this place is tr

I frantically scrolled through PT's texts, to find the abrupt end.

There was a string of texts from my mom, but I ignored it after seeing the odd texts from PB. An attachment that was still loading with several texts behind it.

Just tell me who shit on the table, and I'll save your job. You're better than the others. Enough games. It's impressive, I'll give them that. But I won't stand for it.

They're playing hard to get but I know it's one of them. Don't leave me hanging here. You could maybe even get that office job you talked about.

The lights are off. I don't know what you guys did, knock this shit off.

I can see it. Out of the corner of my eye, I can see it

The image buffered and I clicked on it, and my mind tried to make sense of the shape shown within the camera's blur. Whatever it was—it had been moving fast, fast enough to barely register the security cameras. Like a glimpse frozen between digital time and space.

Caught in the frozen still was the image of something crouching atop the break room table. Bowed legs—two human and two canine—flexed as bloody shit rained down on the table below it. Even in the blurry picture, it looked pained—angry. Amongst the strange limbs was a cluster of faces atop its shoulders, all of them looking in different directions, unable to hold the focus of the camera. A split face of a man with a woman on either side, a look of agony splayed across their faces. Protruding between the two was the gnarled snout of a dog or something like it, its teeth bared angrily, saliva trailing across them.

He did say he was really good with cameras.

SHE WANTED TO SEE GOD

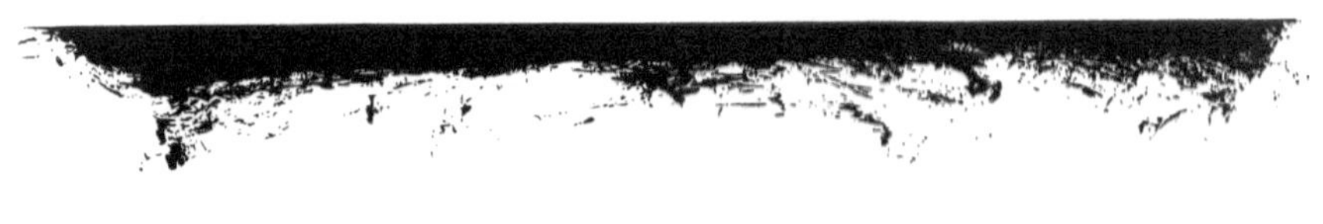

She wanted to see God. I'll never understand why.

I looked over her online dating profile almost nervously, reading her modest bio under the glow of the monitor. I had browsed the app for a time, slowly declining portraits with a lazy swipe of a thumb. Whether the red flags were blatantly obvious, or I had self-fabricated them as I went, I couldn't help but see the potential worst in every selfie I came across. I wish I could say it was the abundance of single moms, the strict height requirement, or the minimum salary desires that drove me away, but it couldn't be further than that.

I don't have any qualms about being a stepdad. I'm 6'2, and in a decent position in my career to potentially provide for an unworking spouse, hell, maybe even own a home. But it wasn't pickiness or shallowness that sueded my constant rejection—it was the fear of what laid behind the charming selfies and angled bikini pics. The potential evil that could lurk behind a smile.

I've been out of the dating scene for... a while. My last relationship had soured in a way that made me consider a life of solitude, TV dinners, and lonely nights with a lotioned hand. Without going into too much detail, the betrayal hurt more than I thought it would, and a part of me wished she would've just been cheating or something.

Anyway, whether I liked it or not, loneliness got the better of me. I found myself once again downloading the forsaken app, the same one that forced me to relocate, file a restraining order, and purchase a handgun that I took to the range once a week as some sort of therapy. I did try conventional counseling as well, but there seemed to be a genuine disconnect between my "irrational fear" and "trauma" that kept me from reaching a notable level of "progress". Despite my gut feeling to keep myself introverted forever, an urge a little further south reminded me how nice it would feel to experience something more than a buffering video and a routine release. I kept telling myself it wasn't worth the hassle, that there wouldn't be a lusty encounter to justify leaving my lonely lif e.

That's when I saw her picture. Pretty and modest, encapsulated by the backdrop of a sunset. Once again out of my league, and once again reading a bio that peaked my interest. Things like **"physical"**, **"energetic"**, and **"outdoorsy"**. I felt a familiar angst within me that soon intertwined a painful memory of a love once lost. Her name was Charlotte, and from the looks of it, she was an avid hiker.

I spent a long time looking at her profile. Nervously chewing at my lip as I read her bio and biting my nails while I scrolled through her photos. In the end, it wasn't her athleticism, flowing blonde hair, or defined thighs that made me linger. It was the note at the bottom of her bio that charmed me the most.

"Looking for someone to explore beautiful things with, if they could keep up."

I swiped with a hint of a smile, before looking down at the pudge of my stomach. I spent most of my days behind a desk and staring at a screen, and would probably die if I attempted a hundred meter dash. But her face looked genuinely *kind,* and I told myself the challenge would be a healthy one. A way to move forward positively and leave the past behind. I figured I had a snowball's chance in hell, anyway.

Until she messaged me the very next day, looking to meet in person.

My last endeavor started innocently at a coffee shop, and I wasn't keen on doing that again. I struggled to come up with a place we could go to break the ice. Before I could suggest anything solid, she proposed we meet at a local park. I thought the idea was great—get some fresh air, *plenty of people around*—until I remembered where my first date with my ex landed me. Out in the open, specifically public, could still lead to something spontaneous. Just the thought of it made me nervous. Before I had the chance to advocate for something else, the date and time was set, and Charlotte would meet me the day after around lunch.

So I sat, waiting anxiously. The park was buzzing, people walking dogs while others sought food from a nearby lunch truck. Time moved in an awkward crawl, and in the back of my mind I wondered if maybe I had jumped the gun—maybe I was trying to get back into the game too soon. The breeze felt too cool on my neck, and my palms felt clammy. I looked around for my date, and saw nothing but other people busy with their own lives. Just as I checked my phone to verify the time, I heard the scuff of approaching sneakers on the pavement. They started to slow, and when I looked for the source, I was met with a set of bubbly, yet determined eyes. It was a jogger, a beautiful blonde clad in a matching set of skin-tight running gear, a sports-bra and leggings that accentuated every defined curve of her body.

"You must be Kevin!" she said, huffing with breath. She slowed to a stop next to me, pausing only to check her watch and stop what I assumed was a timer. As I watched her sweat glisten in the sunshine, I became painfully aware just *how* out of her league I was. Charlotte stood before me, looking every bit like the photos that depicted her on the dating app.

I stood and introduced myself with a far-from-smooth hand-shake, and offered her a seat. She took it, tossing her long ponytail behind her. Her hair was long and well maintained, and she flashed an embarrassed smile of pearly whites.

"I'm so sorry, I didn't expect you to be early. Thought I had time for another lap," she laughed, catching her breath.

I looked at my slacks and polo, and shoes that would probably blister my feet if I tried as much as a jog. I felt like I had walked into some kind of TikTok prank.

"I feel underdressed. If I would've known, I would've dressed more appropriately," I said, wanting to smack myself in the fore-head with each consecutive word that spilled.

"Oh no, it's my fault, really. I should've said something. I exercise every day, and this is the only time I get before work. And I never miss a day," she had a hint of a southern drawl, one that seemed to be slowly overwritten by life in the city "and I thought if I mentioned a run in our messages, you'd probably ghost me. Most guys do," she smiled apologetically.

"Really?" I asked, although I couldn't help but wonder if I would've done the same thing. Running was... intimidating.

She nodded, before checking her watch again. Her brow fur-rowed at the sight.

"Hey," she began, placing a hand on my thigh, "I'd love to get to know you more, but I have one more lap to go. Would you mind if we did it on the go? We can walk it," she smiled, getting up before I could answer. I gave her an of-course-yeah-that-sounds-good as I stood up, already falling behind her. She said walk, but it was definitely a brisk one. I jogged until I was walking beside her, and as the sidewalk passed below us, I got to know Charlotte quickly.

By day, Charlotte was an avid athlete. She was into running, swimming, hiking, rock-climbing—the list went on and on. She had competed in several marathons and did things like running and biking for charity. She explained all of these things with great enthusiasm, fidgeting excitedly as we worked our way through the park. By night, she was an accountant at a severely understaffed firm. This was about as much as she wanted to say about her position, aside from the fact that it sucked the life out of her, keeping it from being where it was supposed to be: outside.

Halfway through the lap, she asked about me, and I filled her in on the boring aspects of my life. What I did for a living. My overall lack of exciting hobbies, and that I was open to the ideas of new ones. She was intrigued by this, and was quick to interject on past experiences. Had I ever gone canoeing? When was the last time I hit a trail? Did I own a bicycle?

I answered each question with the unfortunate truth that I hadn't been active in those particular physical activities in quite some time. I got the feeling I was losing her, that she had met up with a dweeb clearly more suited for online gaming and painting miniatures. Regardless of how embarrassing it felt, I made it clear I was open to new things. It wouldn't be the first time I went way out of my comfort zone.

By the time we made it back to the bench, it couldn't have been more obvious that we were probably incompatible. She seemed indifferent to our conversation, sipping her water and checking her watch again like there was some place she'd rather be. While I braced for the incoming rejection, she startled me with a question:

"So, what do you think?"

"Think about what?" I said, trying to keep cool.

"Hiking. This Saturday. I promise I'll go easy on you," she said, with a hopeful smile. I couldn't believe she was asking *me* for an actual next date.

"Uh... y-yeah! I'd love to. I think I can handle it," I said, attempting to hide my excitement. I didn't think I'd actually go hiking, but I decided I would go wherever she wanted as long as there was a chance of seeing that smile again.

We made the plans then and there. She said she would pick a beginner's trail, and would text me the night prior with a location to meet her at. It all seemed so surreal—her genuine excitement, her flowing blonde hair, her *body*—I don't know if my game was better than I thought or if she was just dying for some company on a trail. One thing I knew for certain; I may have gotten myself in over my head again.

She explained she had to run so she could get ready for work, and that it was nice to meet me. As I watched her go, she spun around and asked a question that felt like a punch to the gut.

"Oh, I'm sorry, but I forgot to ask. What happened with your last relationship?"

A chill went down my spine, and I found myself looking around the park for an answer that wouldn't cause a commotion. When my eyes drifted to a cluster of bushes near the walking path, the hairs on my neck stood up.

"We, uh, well... we felt our lives were going in different directions, I guess," I chuckled, and scratched my head. "What about you?"

"He couldn't keep up," she said simply, before jogging away.

***

I arrived Saturday with new hiking boots, fresh cargos, a new water bottle, and a welling pit of anxiety in my stomach. Charlotte was already there waiting for me, scrolling through her phone behind the wheel of an old Jeep Wrangler. It was a crisp summer afternoon, a cool breeze that blended with the warm sun above.

"I'm surprised you showed," she said, hopping out and meeting me in the gravel lot. She looked me up and down, taking a long look at my obviously brand new boots before smirking.

"I said I'd be here," I assured, taking a moment to admire the forest around us, as well as her outfit. With a string tank-top and short cargo shorts, she looked like a blonde *Lara Croft*.

"This one's not so bad. Only a mile-and-a-half. Think you're up for it?" she said, twirling a lock of blonde hair. She seemed eager and ready to go.

"I won't tap unless you do," I said, with more confidence than I felt.

The trail itself wasn't too bad. Charlotte led the way, each step planted like she was one with the earth. At first I smiled, thinking it was too easy to land a date with someone like her, and all I had to do was go for a *hike.* Watching her hair sway and her thighs work felt like a dream... until I started to feel the burn in my legs. It crept on slowly at first, a slow ache in my thighs, then the alarming strain in my calves. I knew I was out of shape, but the onset fatigue felt pathetic. To my surprise, Charlotte picked up on the struggle I fought so hard to hide.

"Not much of a hiker, are ya?" she said with a giggle, slowing her pace so I could catch up. After 15 minutes, she hadn't even broken a sweat.

"I haven't tapped out yet," I stated, trying not to sound too out of breath. I expected her to be disappointed, regretting asking me on the trip. But instead of sarcasm and deliberate sighs, she started coaching me. Soft little words of encouragement, a trickle of wisdom from someone clearly experienced.

"Next time, you should stretch a little before the hike,"

"I didn't see you stretch," I remarked.

"I didn't need to. I stretch every morning," she smiled.

"Wow. Dedicated."

"Your boots need to be broken in. A couple hikes and they should acclimate pretty well, but you're gonna have blisters for sure. And don't try to trudge angrily, let the path take you. Listen to the trees, the wilderness. Let yourself go,"

My mind drifted to my last first date, the wind in the trees, the sounds of nature. A soft whisper in my ear, and the exhilarating thrill that followed. Once again, out of my element, with a woman more experienced than me. Even though my legs were on fire... I liked it. Our small talk continued over the scuffs of boots on the dirt, and the longer we talked, the more I wanted to know about her.

By the time I was starting to feel like I was getting the hang of it, we arrived back at the parking lot. I looked at her Jeep in amazement; the time had flown. The hike hadn't been so bad after all. After we hydrated and I caught my breath, she leaned against her vehicle and crossed her arms.

"So?" she asked.

"So what?"

"Think you'd be up for another?"

I wanted to puke. "Today?"

"No. Next Saturday. Same time, different trail. I'm swamped with work during the week, but I'm free next weekend. We can do something a little harder next time. Think you can handle it?" she asked, smiling.

"I'd love to. If you don't mind dragging me along again," I said, feeling elated. I was sure I had embarrassed myself beyond saving, yet there she was, wanting me to accompany her again.

"Cool," she held my gaze for longer than I expected, and I couldn't help but hold it as well. After a few silent seconds, she giggled and went in for a hug, which took me by surprise. I was a sweaty mess, but I was afraid of making her feel unwanted. She pulled away quickly, already heading to her Jeep.

"You're gonna be sore as hell. Plenty of ice for your calves and ankles once it sets in. I'd take it easy for a couple days, but I'd also encourage some exercise in between hikes." before I could take offense, she turned and offered a final genuine smile, "You did good today."

"Oh. Thanks! I'll see you next weekend."

And then she was gone, leaving my legs feeling weak, and my heart fluttering.

The work week that followed was miserable. It felt like I had literally ripped both of my calves, and worried I would collapse whenever

I got out of bed in the morning. I followed Charlotte's advice and iced the sore muscles whenever I could, even running a hot bath to soak as they healed. And she wasn't kidding about the blisters; by the time I got home and took off the boots, my heels and pads were covered with swollen lumps. It was hell, but a part of me liked the idea of pushing myself and doing something other than wasting away in front of my computer.

By Wednesday, I took a long hard look at myself in the mirror shirtless, and noticed how flabby I had gotten over the years. I decided if she was serious about taking me with her, I would get serious about getting in shape. I couldn't help but think of what she had said the day we met, about why her last relationship didn't pan out.

He couldn't keep up.

By Thursday, I found myself tucking my feet under the sofa and doing sit-ups for the first time in over a decade. I decided to cut out my nightly beer or two, and replaced it with ice water instead. By Friday, Charlotte texted me to make sure we were still on for another trail, and I sent an enthusiastic text back. That night I ran to the convenience store and bought an expensive set of insoles, a bigger water bottle, and body powder to ward off chafing.

Saturday morning was much like the previous, pulling up to another small parking lot to see her waiting for me. She had picked another local spot, this time on the other side of town, one that seemed to have more overgrowth and steeper inclines. A faded wooden sign at the trail's entrance read: 3mi.

She was wearing another very attractive combo of outdoorsy and athletic, and greeted me with a light side hug. She noticed the bigger water bottle and beamed.

"Came better prepared this time?" she smirked.

"Gotta stay hydrated," I said, really wishing my game was better.

Like last time, Charlotte took the lead. This trail was immediately more challenging, the entrance alone feeling like climbing a set of stairs. My veteran guide took it like it was nothing, and I made a conscious attempt to keep my eyes on the trail and not her attractive figure. The insoles gave me an upper hand, and the fresh powdering kept my chubby thighs from trying to start a fire. I kept up a little better than last time, but she still ended up slowing her pace so I didn't lag too far behind on every incline.

Charlotte didn't divulge much about her personal life, and to be honest, neither did I. It was strange, going on a second "date" with a girl that I found on an app common for "finding and fucking and moving on". Considering how my last relationship went, this was a wildly different change of pace. But it was a *nice* change. She seemed genuinely happy for the company on the trail, and cheered me on when she sensed I was getting winded. We'd stop for breaks occasionally, taking in the scenery around us. Birds chirped, squirrels skittered. And when I found myself looking at her, admiring her smile, her eyes, her pretty blonde hair, I wondered if I was expected to make a move or not. I didn't want to be friendzoned or appear like I lacked the courage to make an advance, but every time we would stop and rest and take a look around, she seemed to be captivated by the environment. Like she was enriched by the fresh air and the swaying trees around us.

Ultimately, I decided I would just go with the flow and follow her lead. There was something magical about being in her company, with nothing but the natural ambience and the sounds of boots on the earth. Just being in her company was... enough.

By the time we reached the end of the second trail, my muscles ached just as they had the last time, and my joints seemed to protest every movement. She cheered as we made it to the parking lot, congratulating me on making it through another route. There was something invigorating about the praise, and the sense of accomplishment warmed me to my core. Even though the trail had to be miniscule compared to what she was used to, I felt a sense of pride for seeing another one through to the end.

It felt good, like I was doing something with my life. Overcoming challenges.

Charlotte reached out for another hug, and we embraced once more. A little longer than the previous, but it still felt nice. Like I was wanted.

I considered asking her out on a lunch date then, but just like the last time, she was already making her way towards her car. Maybe something like that was too soon.

"I'll see you next week?" she asked, keys in hand, her eyes brimming with hope.

"You text me, I'll be there," I remember saying. The smile she gave when she got the response was worth the hours of profuse sweat and cramps. I watched her leave again, already looking forward to the next weekend.

After the first two hikes, the summer passed in a blur. I started taking my fitness seriously, exercising in one way or another each day. In preparation for the hikes to come, I started conditioning myself at the gym, picking workouts that would simulate the experience of future hikes. I drank more water on a regular basis, and swapped lonely nights of gaming and takeout food for meal preps and early nights for plenty of sleep. It wasn't long until I began exploring the world of pre-workout and protein supplements, trying my best to build my body to be able to keep up with Charlotte. I even started getting up earlier every Saturday to stretch and warm up. I had dropped a few pounds in the first week, and started noticing slack in the usual notch I had in my belt.

It was exhausting at first, but the look of admiration I received from Charlotte would only drive me to work harder during the off week between each hike. Four miles, five-and-a-half, then six. They continued to increase in difficulty, until I found myself breezing through the easier portions, sometimes wishing the trail had been more difficult. I wanted to work *harder,* I wanted her to see I was serious. It wasn't long until I was able to keep pace with Charlotte, hiking side by side through miles of towering pine and maple trees, climbing hills that would lead to exceptional views.

But my performance and physique wasn't the only thing growing—Charlotte's overall mood and affection seemed to be changing as well. What used to be an awkward hug would evolve to a kiss on the cheek, and holding hands through the last stretch of the trail. It filled my stomach with butterflies, like I was in high-school again. Not long after that, she would give me a kiss on the lips when we'd first meet, and she'd talk to me more enthusiastically about our time spent in between. It would always seem cold and distant during the work week, only for her to be ecstatic to see me as soon as I would pull into the parking lot of the next park we would conquer together. After the first kiss, I hinted at maybe doing something during the week, maybe grabbing lunch, dinner, or a drink. She would always tell me she was really busy during the week, and she could never find the time to do something other than the weekly Saturday hike.

This saddened me, but I tried not to let it show. I didn't want to come off as clingy, and I started making it a personal rule that I wouldn't engage with her physically unless she initiated contact. I wasn't sure if she had an issue with intimacy or maybe she was still trying to get over her last boyfriend. I tried to keep these thoughts on the backburner, and stay focused on whatever hike we would do next, and my increasingly involved exercise during the week in between.

But as the hikes got lengthier, our chats never went beyond small talk. Whatever she did let me hear was always curt and to the point. She never really got into her past, her upbringing, her life outside of hiking. Even after the sixth trail, the only thing I had learned about her was that her parents had been very strict and religious. Always pushing her to do well in school, enroll in whatever sports she could, and attend church on Sundays. I would later learn this was why her only available day was Saturday, as her devotion to faith and her own physical fitness ate up all of her time outside of work. She later confessed that her parents were no longer around, and she didn't have any relatives to speak to. For the longest time, her only companion in the world had been trails and her own determination.

I continued our silent and mostly private agreement of trails and PG affection, but that changed on the twelfth hike, on one of the last hot days of summer. Ten miles of rugged rock and winding trails, with a peak halfway through that led to a downhill stretch. I had gotten pretty good at keeping pace with her, and when we reached the hill that led to the midway point and a supposedly gorgeous view, we raced to the top.

The view was spectacular. An overlook of miles and miles of multicolored trees, a variety of shades that signaled our ascension into fall. I didn't get the chance to enjoy it for long, because for the first time in our strange two-month relationship, Charlotte threw her arms around me and kissed me in an unexpected wave of passion. Her advance took me off guard, but it didn't stop me from leaning into it. It continued until we retired to a nearby bench, and proceeded to make out for the better part of ten minutes. Our hands explored awkwardly and hesitantly, and I traced the curves of her perfect body through her clothes—until she abruptly had enough. She pulled away without a word, out of breath, and visibly embarrassed. She apologized like she had assaulted me or something, but I reassured her that I was okay with it. It didn't seem to make her feel any better, and she awkwardly pushed off the bench and continued on the trail, leaving me in a painfully aroused stupor. I shook the moment away, readjusted myself quickly and tried to catch up, wondering what exactly had taken place.

It was then, near the end of the longest trail yet, I tried to pry a little. I knew the question was more invasive than our previous ambiguous chats, but after hiking with her for the majority of the summer, I was dying to know more about her. Before I could talk myself out of the question, I grabbed her arm gently and tried to seem nonchalant. I asked what it was that pushed her to do the hikes every weekend.

"What are you looking for? The ultimate view? The biggest challenge? What's your end goal?" I elaborated, trying to smooth over my prying.

Charlotte stopped, and for a moment, she looked at me begrudgingly. I was shocked she was so taken back.

"What, are you tired of this? I thought you were keeping up. Is this too much for you?" she asked, almost accusingly. I felt my cheeks flush with embarrassment, and for the first time, there seemed to be actual trouble in our platonic relationship.

"Oh no, nothing like that! I was just... curious what drives you, is all. You seem very determined. I was just wondering if there was something specific you were looking for. Like a specific trail you wanted to beat, or something like that. I *like* this, and I don't want to fuck it up. I just... want to know what you're looking for. That's it. You don't have to answer, if you don't want to," I defended myself, trying to walk it back. Her explosive change of mood was unexpected, and I tried my best to mend whatever nerve I had struck.

For a moment, she stared daggers into me, and I couldn't help but think I had indeed fucked it up. But then she lowered her gaze, and her expression softened, and she started to contemplate what I asked. She chewed her lip and looked away, standing silently in the breeze as the trees swayed around us. I started to feel guilty, like I had overstepped.

"Look Charlotte, don't worry about it. It's not import—" but she waved her hand, cutting me off. I waited for her to find the words she was looking for, and when she did, they raised the hairs on the back of my neck.

"I want to see God,"

Charlotte left it at that, and continued down the trail, to the parking lot that was nearly in view. I followed close behind, unsure of what to say to such a thing. It didn't make any sense to me, and my mind worked to try to find the appropriate response, one that could repair the damage I had apparently caused from my question. Charlotte didn't say another word on the way to her car, and kept her eyes on the ground as she dug out her keys. It was clear she was done for the day, and didn't plan on saying goodbye.

It felt so surreal. Not long ago she was climbing on top of me on the park bench, grinding herself against me. And now she was about to be gone, possibly for good.

"Charlotte, wait!"

She hesitated as I jogged up to her, her hand resting on the handle of the Jeep's door. She took a deep breath and turned, and I could see tears welling in her eyes. I grabbed her hand and held it in both of mine.

"Look... I'm sorry. I didn't mean to pry. It doesn't matter—just forget what I said, okay? I don't need to know why you want to do this or if there's any kind of end game. I just don't want it to end, that's all. Being with you, going on these hikes, has been the best thing to happen to me in such a long time. I look forward to it all week, and I don't know what I'd do if I couldn't do it again. If this is what you want to do—I don't care how long the trail is—I want to do it with you. I don't want this to end. I wouldn't trade it for anything," I said, and tried my best not to deflate.

She looked up at me, and a single tear ran down her cheek. I gently wiped it with my thumb, before resting a hand on her shoulder.

"You probably think I'm weird, saying what I said."

"No. Not at all," I lied. In truth, I was trying to avoid the subject as best as I could.

"So... same time next week, then?" she asked, with the same look of hope she had in the beginning. She sniffled softly, and there was an inkling of a smile.

"Same time next week," I assured, and she squeezed my hand, before pulling me into a hug. We stood like that for a time, the sun setting and the world darkening around us. She pulled away and kissed me on the lips, before letting me go.

"Okay. I'll see you then," she said, and then she was gone.

I spent the next week working harder than ever before. Despite every exhausted day, I found sleep harder to come by. Each night, I tossed and turned. I couldn't help but replay the words in my head, her strange reason for wanting to go on the trails, as well as her explosive reaction to my question.

I want to see God.

I thought you were keeping up.

They echoed in my head as I pushed in the gym, running mile after mile on the treadmill and doing sit-ups until I thought I would throw up. The more I tried to make sense of it, the more confused I became. At first, I thought there was some kind of religious angle, and I wondered if I should ask to go to church with her. Then I wondered if it was some kind of unique runner's high, and it was all about pushing her to her absolute limit as an athlete. After that I pondered if it was some kind of sexual thing, and I'll admit it pushed me down a research rabbit hole of how to give her the most intense orgasm of her life. All these thoughts felt silly in the end, and I was left worrying that I had missed the point and fucked the whole thing up entirely.

I felt obsessively drawn to my phone, keeping it near me at all times just in case she texted or called. Despite her saying she would see me next weekend, I couldn't help but feel like I had jeopardized the good thing we had going. I was kept up by my own thoughts at night, haunted by her hurt tone in her voice after I asked about the hiking. All I had to do was go with the flow as usual, and I just had to open my mouth.

There were no friendly pleasantries throughout the week, no small talk over the next trail. I had gotten accustomed to how much she was warming up to me, and the connection felt like it had suddenly become cold. Just when I began to wonder if she had decided to move on from me, I received a text Friday evening.

> 8am. Two-mile hike. Don't be late.

As I froze and read the text repeatedly, she sent another with the address. I clicked on the link to see it was another trail I had never been to, but this time it was in the next town over. I was shocked that the hike was much shorter than the previous one, but I paid it no mind. I would be there on time, and I would do my best to make her feel better.

The next morning, I was surprised to find there wasn't a parking lot for the next trail. The GPS took me to an easily missable gravel road, one that led into a dense pack of trees. Fall's influence was in full swing now, and I could barely make out the path through the layers of discarded orange leaves. It didn't seem like the typical place we'd go, and it felt like I was driving into private property. All of my caution went out the window however, when I saw the familiar Jeep parked at the dead end, with a beautiful woman leaning against it. There was something different this time, something that twisted my stomach in a nervous knot.

Charlotte wasn't wearing her typical combo of tank-top and leggings with a ponytail. Her usual getup was replaced by a colorful sundress and jean jacket, and her hair was let down. She had her usual hiking boots on, but my attention was pulled to the sheer amount of smooth, toned legs. My stomach fluttered with butterflies, and my hands shook against the keys as I shut off the car. I took a deep breath, and got out of the car.

"You look incredible, I feel so under-dressed!" I said, shouldering the pack I had come accustomed to bringing. The cool autumn air chilled the nervous sweat on my neck.

"The weather's really nice, and I wanted a break from the same old thing. Plus, this trail is special," she said, with a devious smirk.

"Oh?" I asked, looking past her. Whatever the trail was, I couldn't see it beneath the recent shed of leaves.

"Yeah. I've never brought anyone out here. There's something I want to show you. You think you can handle it?" she asked. She seemed nervous, giddy even. As happy as I was that she had cheered up since we last went out, I couldn't help but feel anxious. There was a familiar dread welling in my stomach, but I dismissed it as paranoia.

"I think I can handle that," I said, trying to keep cool. Charlotte beamed, and greeted me with a soft kiss. I melted against it.

"Let's go, handsome. It shouldn't take long," she said, taking my hand in hers. I followed obediently, her remark making my heart race just as quickly as I felt the need to fall to my knees and vomit.

Handsome.

The trail was a steady incline, but nothing compared to the recent hikes we had been through. It felt like a dream. I was in the best shape I had ever been, being pulled along by a girl from my dreams, all the while lured in by the cozy scent of fall and Charlotte's intoxicating perfume. I was entranced by the rhythmic crunch of leaves under our boots, and the occasional smile I would catch Charlotte giving me. It felt warm and entrancing. It felt like *love.*

Charlotte didn't speak on our trek, and neither did I. I had fumbled on the last hike, and I wanted to be sure I didn't make the same mistake again. Lost in the scenery and lost in her, I followed obediently like a curious dog on a leash. Whenever I was unsure of the mysterious trail, Charlotte would pull me along, guided by her own unseen compass.

It didn't take us long to reach the destination. We arrived at a small clearing in the forest, the orange fronds falling serenely like petals on the breeze. Charlotte let go of my hand and let me walk on my own as I marveled at the little spot. The air felt cooler, carrying with it the calming ambience like waves on the ocean. As I looked around in my euphoria, my eyes settled on something that stood out from the otherwise perfect expanse. At first I thought it was the massive root system of a fallen tree, the way it stood frozen near the outer edge of the undisturbed leaves. But the longer I looked, the more I couldn't help but notice the familiar shapes in the cluster of twisted wood.

It was an altar, made entirely of carved hands.

There was a heavy ruffle on the leaves, and I gave a startled look at Charlotte. She had shed her jean jacket, and let it fall to the forest floor.

"Charlotte?" I asked, nervously clutching the straps on my pack. Her cheeks were rosy, and her eyes said more than any words possibly could. She held her gaze on me, even as she bent down to unlace her boots, one by one.

"When's the last time you felt the earth beneath your feet?" she asked, almost a whisper. I watched her take off her boots, nudging them together neatly before pulling off her socks. I was overwhelmed by the casual exposure of her feet, her painted toe nails. They matched the color of her dress.

"I don't know," I stammered, my thoughts twisting with the reminder of mud against my skin, and my hot breath against the interior of a mask.

"Will you join me?" she asked, speaking slowly as she tucked her socks into her boots. I couldn't help but watch, my breath shuddering as she flexed her toes and stood amongst the leaves. As she reached under her skirt and gently pulled down her underwear. I watched until it fell to her ankles, and she stepped out of them.

"Yes,"

I don't remember sliding the pack off my shoulder. I remember fumbling with the laces of my boots, jerking the double-knots until they unspooled and I could get my feet out. My hands shook as I pulled at the socks, listening to the soft crunch as Charlotte's bare feet worked their way towards mine. She moved gracefully, inno-cently, lustfully. I felt the earth beneath my feet, the soft crinkles on my skin. She wrapped her arms around my neck and kissed me slowly, passionately. When she bit at my lip, her breath was warm and seductive. She kissed my neck, and my hands traveled the soft fabric of her dress, exploring every immaculate curve. As I thought of what was underneath it, she whispered in my ear.

"I want you to lay down now."

My mind raced, my heart pounded, and my arousal fought against the inside of my cargos. I sat in front of the altar of carved hands, trying to ignore how uncomfortable it made me. Charlotte helped me out of my shirt, her fingers warm against the scrawl of goosebumps. She tossed it away and gently pushed me down, placing her hands on my chest as she climbed on top of me. Her hands trembled just like mine, and as I watched her unfasten the button and pull at the zipper, I became aware of how solid the ground felt beneath me. The crush of leaves. An overgrowth of moss. Below, the unmistakable solitude of a stone slab.

Above, the wind breathed through the trees. Charlotte bit her lip as she felt my girth in her hand, feeling the stiffness that grew until it hurt. She hunched over me and kissed me once more, and as she turned to bite my neck, I felt my eyes drifting toward my pack on the ground. Through my melting thoughts, I realized the lack of a condom.

"Charlotte, I didn't bring any—"

She silenced me with a finger and leaned back, holding the finger there as she positioned herself above me. The other hand guided me towards the wet kiss, and the warm embrace that took my breath away. As I held my breath and grabbed fistfuls of her skirt, she tensed as she absorbed me. My legs shifted, and I felt the earth beneath my feet, and Charlotte's steady breathing turned to a pained wince. As her hips met mine, a sensation reminded me of an awkward time I had when I was in high-school, in the back seat of my car. The unforgettable feeling of a hymen tearing.

"Charlotte, were you—" her hand clamped around my mouth and she started working her hips, grinding against me despite my protest. I felt a twinge of guilt as I enjoyed her dominance, despite learning this was her first time. Trying to speak between her fingers, I grabbed her by the hips and tried to slow her down. She didn't need to go this rough, we could take our time, *she* could take her time—

Charlotte pressed hard on my chest and pushed herself up, gyrating slowly as she worked the straps of her dress down her shoulders, revealing breasts and a defined stomach. She grabbed my wrists firmly and made me take them in my hands, moaning against my thumbs as they ran over tender spots. Before I could protest any further, she rode harder, planting her hands once more on my chest. My fingers explored and ran down her stomach until they rested firmly on her hips, this time giving in completely. I worked my legs out of my shorts and kicked them away, baring everything as Charlotte had her way with me.

Every soft moan and each shuddered breath pushed me further past the point of no return, and before I knew it, I was pulling her into me, greedily working with her. I could feel it coming, each movement grinding me into the stone below as I whispered I was close.

In a final act of ownership, Charlotte grabbed my wrists and pinned them to the earth, riding as hard as she could. I thought of the hikes and the struggles of each mile, and the tensions it brought with her increasing affection. Every soft kiss, every gentle embrace leading to this intimate union. I thought of the coming release, and surrendered to her completely, eager to release everything I had built up.

Charlotte moaned. I squeezed my eyes shut. And my hands contorted just like the ones on the altar above me.

Charlotte shuddered as I spasmed beneath her, and I groaned with relief as the product of my love flooded into her. Her breath came in huffs, labored exhales against the hair in her face. She giggled softly as the feeling faded, and I looked up at her with blurry vision. She kissed me again, her hands releasing me and digging into the leaves at our sides.

The words she spoke felt sobering in the chill of the forest.

"Thank you. Thank you for keeping up, and sharing this moment with me," she said, her voice tired, almost somber.

I was trying to find the words, but my emotions struggled to compute it all. It came in flashes, and my brain couldn't process it quickly enough. The altar, her virginity, the orgasm, the blade—

She had pulled it from the leaves, the steel sharp and wicked. I didn't understand why it had been hiding there, why she had it in the first place. I mumbled in desperation, a plea that couldn't quite take flight. Even as she clutched the blade in both hands and raised it high above. When she spoke again, the words shook my soul.

"I'll cherish it forever."

Charlotte brought the blade down and I screamed, my entire body tensing against the incoming tip of the blade. I squeezed my eyes shut and waited for the pain, but it never came. I had expected extreme pain, but the only thing I could feel was a hot trickle pooling over me. I opened my eyes to see Charlotte hunched over, still holding the dagger, the blade disappeared into her stomach. She looked at me and smiled weakly, just as she would when we'd complete a hike. Before I could stop her, she pushed it further and twisted, a groan of agony escaping her lips as the wound ripped and s purted.

"No! No-no-no-no!"

There was so much blood, too much blood, and Charlotte gripped the hilt for dear life as the color drained from her face. The wind stopped, the blood soaked, and above us the hands on the altar began to move. The digits squirmed and popped, shaking away years of dust and dirt as they each interlocked and made symbols in unison.

"Charlotte, please, no—"

I looked to find her still, frozen, the light fading from her eyes. The scream that followed was horrible, a gurgling groan that erupted from her mouth in a rush of hot blood. It splashed over me in bursts, and as my eyes welled with tears, I watched as a collection of hands worked their way out of her throat. Two. Four. Eight. Her jaw broke and her cheeks split to accommodate for the arms that followed, demonic appendages stained in red that reached for my throat, my face, my hair. I bucked wildly underneath her, sobbing until all I could muster was a continuous wail. I slipped and fell in the soaked leaves, thrashing to escape what had become of Charlotte.

She whipped around to see me, her pained howl of a voice gurgling as her bloodshot eyes found me. They stared lazily before they exploded outward, the pupils replaced by the crooked fingers that flexed and squeezed out of her sockets. Her dress still hung from her hips, and her new form made no effort to fix it. Her defined stomach pulsed a deep purple, a plague of bruising that soon gave way to an impossible addition of greedy, grasping limbs. Her head seemed too heavy to hold up, and when she toppled over, the many limbs caught and balanced her. Several of them bent at the elbow and held her up, like a centipede rearing back to show its feeler s.

Horribly disfigured, Charlotte started to produce a series of sounds, and in and out of two syllables that echoed from her swollen throat. She repeated it over and over, staring with open palmed hands where her eyes should be.

Kevin.

Tears welled as I reached down, pawing blindly until I felt the strap of my pack. I squeezed it until my nails dug into my skin. My only response came in the form of a panicked mumble, one I chanted over and over as she tried to call out to me.

"I'm sorry."

I ran. I heard it give chase, but I don't know how fast. My legs pumped as fast as they could as I scrambled naked down the path, my thoughts racing between Charlotte behind me and the pack in my hands, the pack that held my phone, my car keys. I continued down the hill in a wild sprint, branches whipping my skin and rocks ripping at my soles. I ran until all my breath came in rasps and my lungs burned with dry fire. I couldn't hear it following, but I didn't dare stop, didn't even think about it until I saw my car come into view.

My heart ached as I passed Charlotte's Jeep, its stark white paint standing out amongst the many shades of orange. I gasped for air as I unzipped the pack and fumbled through it, tossing away packs of granola, jerky, and water bottles until I found the only two things my mind could make sense of. My phone, and my keys.

I started the car and backed out in a panic, kicking up gravel and sticks and nearly crashing into a tree as I tore out of the hidden gravel and swung my car back onto the road, ignoring the blaring horns of oncoming traffic. My tires squealed until they found purchase and I kept driving, working on autopilot with no real plan or direction in mind. It wasn't until I was miles out of town that it hit me, the beautiful woman that had taken me to the altar in the middle of nowhere. The beautiful woman that had seen God.

I sobbed and beat at the steering wheel as the miles passed beneath me, unsure of where to go and what to do. I cried in the dead silence, mourning the impossible loss and the fear of the unknown. The images haunted me as I drove, the clearing, the many twisted hands. I could hear her scream playing on a loop.

Thank you for keeping up.

I'll cherish it forever.

It wasn't until the sun began to set that the reality of it all began to set in. The scene that I had fled. The evidence I had left behind. My clothes, my DNA. If I called the cops, it didn't matter if they believed my ravings or not, the forest would paint a pretty damning picture.

Regardless if she ran away and they never found *her,* someone would find her Jeep eventually. Someone would connect the dots.

I don't know how long I had been driving when the fuel light came on. I didn't even know what town I was in. Under the cover of nightfall, I pulled into a gas station, parking on the side of the building away from the lights of the pumps.

I left her there, alone. She called out to me, and I left her there.

No gas, no money, no clothes. I know I need to go back. I know she's still out there, roaming those woods. *Looking for me.*

It needs to be dealt with. I can't leave her there alone. I need help. I need someone who would understand, someone who would know what to do and wouldn't go to the police.

I look at her number, wondering *why* I never deleted it from my contacts. I don't know why I saved it. But I'm glad I did.

The dial tone drums in my ear, and a familiar voice picks up on the second ring. She almost sounds… happy to hear from me. Like she always knew I'd call. When I finally speak, my voice is dry and weak.

"Mona?"

THE DEER STAND

My morning was ruined in the form of a red pickup truck. I had just put the coffee on when I heard the rumble of an old engine, and I looked out the front window to see it making its way down the drive.

It was just after 6 am., the sun barely breaking over the horizon. 6 am, on a Saturday, nonetheless. I had just finished my move into a new house, trying to put things back together through the wreckage of a far-from-pleasant divorce. After months of paperwork and back and forth my nightmare float of a failing marriage amidst the horrible housing market was finally over, and this was my first weekend to take a load off and enjoy it.

Until the truck pulled in. A slow coast, in a way someone would arrive at their grandmother's house. Almost making themselves at home. I stood there for a while in disbelief, taking in the faded paint and rusted rocker panels of their crew cab as it sauntered in.

At first, I hoped the truck was just trying to turn around. But instead of swinging in front of the garage and backing away, the vehicle slowed to a stop, and a man got out. I wanted to scowl. I could already feel the random visitor spoiling my coffee and sunrise, and the way he trounced to the front door, almost excitedly, confused me more than anything.

He looked to be in his mid-fifties, dressed in layers of denim and Carhartt. There was a giddy excitement to his walk, like he couldn't wait to get to the door. The way he waltzed up the gravel—he certainly wasn't lost.

It was too early for a salesman, or someone spreading the good word. This person was sure they were supposed to be here, *comfortable* in the thought they were in the right place. I couldn't help but head to the door, despite the odd discomfort I felt from such an early visitor. I lurked in the dark and opened the screen door, watching them practically bounce up the steps. Through the little glass window, I watched them straighten their jacket, smooth their mustache, and raise a fist to knock on the door.

Before they could rap their knuckles, I opened it. Their look of genuine excitement faltered immediately, replaced by a confused apprehension. Their jolly demeanor melted before me like a costume falling away.

"Can I help you?" I asked, a little abrasive.

The man froze, fist still posed, his eyes frantically looking me up and down, then past me. I shuffled to block his view.

"U-Uh—hey, hello there!" he exclaimed awkwardly, straightening himself. Despite his quick transition into *the friendly neighbor*, there was an odd agitation nipping at him. When I didn't say anything, he cleared his throat.

"Is uh—is Rodger home? I wasn't aware he'd have company today," he fidgeted for a moment, before making a clear effort to stand more still.

"Oh, I'm really sorry to be the one to tell you—Rodger passed away a few months ago. I just recently closed up on the home and moved in," I said awkwardly.

The man looked like I was playing a prank on him at first, his mouth opening in preparation of the laugh. The confused apprehension washed over quickly, replaced by a look of genuine loss.

"Oh. You're serious?"

"Unfortunately, I am. He left no will, and the realtor checked repeatedly for next of kin, but... it looked like he left no family behind. I'm sorry for your loss,"

"Wow. *Wow,* this is really unexpected. He uh, he always seemed to be in such good health, in such high spirits. I can't believe it. He was a *dear* friend, we went way back."

I nodded sympathetically, but couldn't help but think of the picture I had seen of the previous owner. He looked every bit of a haggard "80".

The man scratched his head and cleared his throat, and for a moment, his eyes darted off to the left of me, like he was trying to see through the house. I followed his gaze and saw nothing but the faded siding and drawn curtains. Was he trying to look through the windows?

"Sorry to hear, friend. Realtor said he was a good guy, really active in the community. Feeding the homeless, stuff like that. Lost a good one, for sure," I said, really wanting to just close the door and be done. But I couldn't quite find the words to respectfully dismiss him.

The man chewed his lip for a moment before returning his attention to me.

"Ah, yeah. He could really *run* with the young'uns. Always seem to keep in touch with his youth, that rascal," he said with a grin, before offering his hand, "name's Clint."

I shook it reluctantly. "Nice to meet you."

"Say," he was already continuing, "the reason I come up here, was for huntin'. Roger would let me use his deer stand out back, past the field. He was a bit of a mentor to me, actually. Taught me all I know," he said, placing a hand over his heart. Like some sort of pledge.

"Oh yeah?" I said, raising my eyebrows, deliberately sighing on the inside. I knew where this was going.

"If you wouldn't mind, could I by chance use the ol' deer stand again? I won't mosey around the property, I swear. Just for a few hours. I already got my tags and everything!" he said, perking up.

I took a deep breath. Behind me, the coffee pot beeped. If I didn't squash this now, it would continue to be a thorn in my side. Perhaps forever.

"Actually, I'm gonna have to tell you no, friend. Sorry for the inconvenience," I said, watching all of his enthusiasm melt in an instant.

"I beg your pardon? It was a *three-hour drive.* I'm just asking for a little courtesy here. Having already made the trip," he said, barely keeping composure. It was like I had slapped him.

"I'm sorry for the inconvenience—"

"*Inconvenience?* I've been coming here to hunt for years. YEARS!" His voice echoed in the early morning, I found myself holding the doorknob tighter.

"Yes, I understand that—"

"No, I don't think you do. This is all I got, outside of work. I'm not asking the world, here. You won't even know I'm there. I can just go back to the stand, sit for a couple hours, then I'll be on my way."

I felt kind of shitty, looking into his pleading eyes, knowing I was going to tell him no. But the way I looked at it, if I gave in now, he would be back. Who knew how many "for old time's sake" there would be?

"The thing is, I can't let you use the deer stand. Because that's what *I'm* going to do," I said, trying to keep straight.

"You're kidding," he said through clenched teeth, his hands curling into fists. Behind the quickly fading mask of kindness, I could see a kindling rage.

"Yeah. Already put the coffee on. Going out in just a moment, actually. Was about to get dressed," I lied, hooking a thumb to the kitchen. Clint's eyes glazed over as he glanced toward the kitchen, before turning back to me with a blank face. He held the look for an uncomfortable amount of time.

"*Bullshit,*" he said, staring me down. I decided I had run out of fake kindness as well.

"Look old man, you can either get off my fucking property, or I can call the police, and they can escort you *three hours* back home."

"Rodger would be rolling over in his grave—" he started, then stopped as I pulled out my phone.

"Choice is yours," I said, punching in the three numbers.

Clint backed down immediately, throwing his hands up like I was overreacting. He did the same slow walk back to his truck, a disgusted scowl letting me know I had wronged him unfairly. By the time he reached for the door of his vehicle, I closed the front door and locked it, only to creep into the next room and peep out the window discreetly. The phone never left my hand.

The angry old man started his truck and sat there for a moment, defeated and dead eyes boring into my house with a blank expression. When he started to scream, I couldn't help but feel goosebumps. Clint beat the steering wheel with hatred and shouted as loud as he could, and I watched in silence as his eyes popped to the point of bursting. He tore out of the driveway then—tires eating at the gravel and spinning out until he made it to the main road, all the while shouting his unheard insults.

I felt uneasy even after he was gone. Walking to the kitchen, I could still feel his lingering rage, and as I poured a cup of coffee, I couldn't help but feel a chill. The strangest thing of all—even though he arrived alone, it looked like he was yelling at the *back seat.*

The deer stand looked to be barely standing. Erected at the wood's edge, the thing was a nightmare of old lumber, rusted nails, and frayed plywood. It looked like it might've been nice at some point, but the years against the elements and lack of repair were starting to show. The longer I looked at it, the less I wanted to actually get i n.

When I saw the deer stand from the house, it didn't look too bad—aside from how it creepily lurked just outside the treeline. The only opening was the side entrance and a rectangular viewport in the front—like a little box under a slanted roof to help with the rain runoff. I had never been much for hunting, but the stand gave me a cozy tree house vibe I hadn't felt since I was a kid.

Against my better judgment, I readjusted the sling for my shotgun and started climbing the rungs.

The old wood groaned against my weight. Once inside, I could hear the wind whistle through the cracks, giving me a chill as I looked around the inside. The walls were covered in markings, some in marker, others carved in. A single black folding chair sat in front of the viewport, and as I ducked in, I helped myself to a seat. The deer stand groaned in response. When I swiveled around to get comfortable, my boots scattered little things at my feet.

The floor was littered with spent ammunition—spent shotgun shells, rifle casings of all sizes, even torn strands of arrow fletching. Over a hundred rounds had been fired and never picked up. I'd have to make a note to clean that up later if I didn't decide to tear the damn thing down.

The scrawling along the wall was interesting as well. I got the impression they were celebratory carvings and such to commemorate kills, even going as far as giving a nickname above the date. The dates themselves were all over the place, with no rhyme or reason.

Tracy (10-12-03)
Silver (1-05-98)
Toothless (11-29-05)

The dates went on and on. Nicknames like "Big Bertha" and "Fucking Bitch". Two different sets of handwriting, permanent marker, paint sticks, knife etching. Whoever had been making notes had been doing it since before I was *born.*

I looked away from the scrawl and unslung the shotgun, propping it up on the viewport. It was a Remington 870 SuperMag, a gift I'd received from my father well over a decade ago. My career as an outdoorsman could be chalked up to a hunter's education course I took when I was a kid. I still had the sense to run a questionable bore snake through it and load it with a handful of slugs, but propping it up now felt silly. Dust still clung in the places where my half-assed wipe down had missed, and I didn't even know if the scope was sighted in.

In my defense, I had never planned on *actually* hunting. More making a show of it. It's not like I expected Clint to come back. It kind of felt like I was marking my territory. And it seemed like a better idea than sitting inside and doom scrolling on my phone.

A cold wind blew across the fields, the mangled remains of last year's bean crops shifting around me. Farmers had worked both sides of the property I now owned, another thing I had already planned to stop as the new owner. Shrugging against the chill, I leaned into the scope and started surveying my property.

I looked at my house, so clear through the scope I could look through my own windows. The thought was creepy, knowing if I had let Clint back here, he could've watched me all morning. With a gun accurate enough to hit me from here, no less.

Unfortunately, most of the actual yard I had was clearly in front. Grass, deer stand, then the trees, with the rising and fall of farmed films on either side. Getting bored quickly, I started to roam, panning the scope horizontally until the scenery turned to a long blend of ruined bean stalks. Just as I wondered if I *should* actually look for a deer, something caught my eye. At first, I thought I had imagined it since I had never seen anything but the fields when I first toured the property.

About a half mile away just over the hill, I could see the little roof of a shack, sticking out amongst a cluster of dead trees. I stared at it for a while, wondering what someone would use such a thing for. And what I could potentially use for it, since it was on my property. There wasn't another house for over a mile, and the placement of it felt... strange.

Being as early as it was, I decided I would go check it out.

Shouldering the gun once more, I climbed out of the rickety deer stand and started in the direction of it. From the ground, you couldn't even see it, and I had never spotted it from the road in all my trips during the move. It was like it was built to be tucked out of sight.

I cursed the cold assaulting my face, but thanked it for the ground under my boots. If it had been just a little warmer, the mud would've made the trek exhausting. I took a moment to admire the scenery as I walked, kicking at the broken beanstalks while the trees loomed in the distance. I liked it out here, and soon I started to have pleasant thoughts of a summer breeze, and how green the forest would look when the leaves returned.

That was, until I saw the truck.

Clint's red pickup was parked in front of the little structure, and he was nowhere to be found.

What the fuck?

I felt for my phone immediately, pulling a glove off before unlocking the screen. Service was practically nonexistent, and I found myself looking back in the direction of the house. It looked much smaller than I anticipated; I had walked longer than I thought.

I decided I would just confront him here; maybe he had some belongings here, and our conversation had gotten heated before he could come clean about it. I tried to keep the sinister thoughts away and give him the benefit of the doubt. Either way, if I could confront him here and get him to leave, this would hopefully be the last I saw him.

Approaching the truck, I felt aware of the gun's dead weight. Part of me wanted to be holding it.

"Clint?" I called, my voice feeling weak in the expanse of the field. Only the wind answered. I started towards the door and stopped, my eyes drifting down to the fluttering glass below the shack's door.

There was a trickle of blood in the grass, a bright red pattering that stood out in the sunlight. The trail continued up the door itself, and when the other details started to pour in, I felt my stomach twist into knots.

The door to the shack was covered in faded scratch marks. It swayed in the wind, leaving nothing but a dark room within. Laying in the grass was a rusted padlock, along with the latch that had broken away from the wood. Someone had bashed it until it broke open.

I looked toward my house, so far in the distance. I could run back, but it would be around ten minutes before I could get the police on the phone. As I mulled it over in my head, a noise echoed from within the shack and carried over the hills.

It was a scream. A woman's, from the sound of it.

Staring into the dark of the shack, I unslung the shotgun and racked the pump, readying a slug in the chamber. Clicking off the safety with my thumb, I felt sick to my stomach. Whoever it was, they sounded terrified.

Using the shotgun's long barrel, I held the door open. Daylight poured into the inside, cutting through a haze of dust. The cramped walls of the shack were lined with shelves of junk—jars of nails, old coffee cans, and tools so corroded they were fused to the wood. The smell came next, a rot so heavy it flooded my lungs, and I gagged. Looking through the dust, I could see the source, just as another scream assaulted my ears.

There was an open hatch in the corner, with a rug tossed to the side. The scream died out, and I was left staring at it, the wind whistling as the gun shook in my hands. I checked my phone again, this time out of desperation. No service. Looking down, I could see nothing but the start of a rusted ladder leading to darkness. I would have to go in.

Choking back another gag, I gingerly knelt and started down the ladder, holding the gun muzzle up as I made the descent. My legs shook as my feet reluctantly found purchase, each step engulfing me in the world below the hatch. When the soles of my shoes finally touched earth, I felt the crude crunch of gravel on stone. The corridor underground only ran one way—narrowly into what would be an empty field above. The only light in the tunnel was a candle every twenty feet, a nearly blind descent into what I could only think was well.

With a final look at the light above, I swallowed hard and started creeping down, the shotgun pointing ahead. I considered using my phone for light, but considering how my hands were shaking, I didn't think I could mentally handle juggling both it and the firearm.

Slow, steady steps. I could hear a whimpering ahead, followed by the jingle of what sounded like chains. I kept pushing through the dark, clutching the gun so tight my fingers hurt. After what felt like an eternity pushing forward, the tunnel opened up to a dimly lit expanse. More candles, just enough to see the horror I had been dreading the whole time.

A woman was lying on the floor, her wrists collected before her in a wrap of chains. The chains were attached to an iron loop bolted into the floor, secured together by a padlock. Her clothes were heavily stained, and I could barely make out the outline of a hooded sweatshirt and leggings. I approached slowly, haunted by the fact Clint was nowhere to be seen. The woman looked at me weakly, and when she tried to scurry away, I held a finger to my lips. She stopped, but continued to look at me wildly with one eye. The other one had been horribly bruised and was swollen shut.

"Are you alright?" I asked, foolishly. She shook her head.

"Where is he?"

She shrugged and mumbled something that sounded like *generator.*

I tried the chains, like I could magically free her without a key. I was sweating, my hands continued to shake as I scrambled around with no plan. I looked at the shotgun and asked a question I didn't want to know the answer to.

"Does he have a gun?" I whispered, and she shook her head again. Her head lolled to the side, like she was trying not to fall asleep. The word she mouthed made me want to vomit.

Worse.

It was then I noticed her hands—the source of the heavy stains. There was a hole in each of her palms, nearly the size of quarters.

In the distance, I heard the cough and squeal of a generator, followed by a blinding light. Strings of bulbs illuminated the tunnel, illuminated more unspeakable horror. A corridor of stone stained almost entirely red. Cages with withered contents, tools hanging from nails, discarded clothing. The sudden light kicked up a flurry of flies, and the buzzing made my skin crawl.

None of that mattered now.

My mind raced for a solution. I didn't have the key for the lock, and I didn't want to leave her alone to go find it. After a moment of panic, I stood and told the woman to cover her ears. She shook her head at first, but when she saw me raise the gun, she pressed her fingers over them and clamped her eyes shut. The ringing was instantaneous, a deafening snap so loud I didn't even feel the gun kick. The padlock exploded along with a chunk of the ground, and the chains started to unravel with the slack. I helped the woman out of the chains and up, all the while repeating the same two phrases through my shattered hearing. I was holding my phone out to her. At some point, it slipped into her open hands.

RUN.

GET OUT OF HERE.

The woman must've gotten the message, as she started immediately for the ladder. I watched with a hint of relief, her silent silhouette getting further away as I got my bearings. As happy as I was that the slug had freed her, the feeling faded as quickly as it came. If I hadn't pulled the trigger, I would've heard him coming. I would've heard the drill.

The pain was unimaginable, and the sensation of my flesh swirling inside and away from me all at once was tenfold what I felt in my ears. I could feel the rumble in my throat, but I couldn't hear my scream, and for a moment I swung the gun wildly to save myself. I felt the barrel knock something hard, and the drill bit angled through the fat in my side before pulling away. I felt for the damage and felt the hot gush on my fingers, at the agonizing spout that had been bored into my "love-handle". I spun around to find him, my hands working desperately to cycle the gun. In the ringing hell, I felt the motion and smelled the dance of gun smoke.

Clint was leaning against the wall, one hand clutching his temple, but it wasn't his face. His face was not a wolf's but *wolves*. Several blood-stained pelts, snouts, and empty eyeholes brought to a point in the center—a homemade nightmare of a mask. At some point, he had shed his clothes, and his only other belonging appeared to be a large cordless drill at his side, still spinning with my blood.

A drill that was pointing at me as he charged again.

I didn't think. I just pulled the trigger. The shotgun bucked at my hip, and the ringing intensified immediately. Clint's hand and the drill exploded together, a burst of red sparks and fingers that brought him to his knees. He held the twisted stump in front of him like an offering, holding it up before peeling the mask from his head.

His face was pained, and he was shouting, but there was only ringing for me. It seemed like he was begging, trying to reason, trying to appeal in some way, but I couldn't keep my eyes on his frail body, his teary eyes. All I could see was the horror and gore around him, the disturbing evidence of a foul, *foul hobby*.

My hands worked on their own, feeding the final slug into the dusty shotgun. Clint waved wildly, shouting something I didn't need to hear. As the barrel level with his head, I thought of the woman, and hoped she made it up the ladder. I pulled the trigger, and the waving stopped.

My head was splitting in two. I couldn't remember climbing up the ladder, but I remember not having to help her up. I remember the feeling of blood cold on the wind, trickling down a soaked pant leg and both ears. I remember seeing the flashing lights and being unable to hear them.

It wasn't until I woke up in the hospital that I could recall what had actually happened. There were over a dozen badges from several counties waiting for me to wake up. Waiting for my statement. It wasn't until they repeatedly confirmed my identity that they told me what had happened.

They told me the woman, who I found out to be "Brittney Carlson", had made it to the road by the time the police arrived. She was barely standing by the time they arrived, and kept urging the police to save the hunter—the *good* one—not the bad one. I guess she had been abducted three towns over when Clint was on his way to visit his dear friend Rodger. Judging by what forensics had found in the tunnel, this had been an annual ritual for the two of them for a long, long time.

"The tunnel" was nearly thirty acres long, comprising various passages and rooms, "fun rooms" according to some of the texts and logs left behind over the years between the two friends. It's rumored Rodger had started excavating it as early as the seventies, given his capabilities in landscaping, vast private property, and standing in the community. Despite the amount of cold missing persons cases in the neighboring states, Rodger was never considered a suspect, and was often seen as the "loving, caring, grandfatherly type" despite never having children of his own.

"Clinton Maybrook" was found to be a resident of Wellington, Florida, a sixteen-hour drive away. He had made the same drive annually in his red pickup, across several routes that were flagged in possible abduction cases over the last twenty years. He was a janitor at a local high school in the area, and was often referred to as "cagey" and "high-strung" by his coworkers, and had been reprimanded twice for misconduct with both students and staff.

I had to go over the story with the police several times. Most of it was happenstance, really, right place at the wrong/right time sort of thing. I could tell I was considered to be a potential accomplice for a while, but with the amount of damning evidence found against Rodger and Clint, the physical evidence of my presence, and the surviving victim's testimony, I've been cleared for some t ime.

It took them some time to go over the tunnel completely. At some point, I got used to seeing the lights and crews out there at night, but I never bothered to go back. I don't plan on ever stepping foot over there either, and as soon as I'm allowed, I'm going to have the whole thing demolished. As far as the deer stand, a sledgehammer and a bonfire made quick work of it.

Last I heard, there were 78 confirmed bodies found in the tunnel, ranging from ages 15-45. It's being rumored that all abductions were from out of state and brought to Rodger's property, where they would poach them from the deer stand like animals. I kept up with it on the news for a while, but once they started discussing the field dressing tools they started finding, I eventually stopped in an attempt to maintain some sanity.

Although I'm mostly healed, I still hear the ringing sometimes. The shotgun was eventually released to me once I was cleared of any charges, and I now keep it clean, oiled, and loaded by the door at all times. I haven't had any shady visitors since, but I feel there might come a day when I'll need it again.

The ringing is mostly gone, but there's some damage that I think will be permanent. A "light tinnitus" they say, but it doesn't help me sleep at night. Sometimes I wake up in the middle of the night and mistake it for a drill.

ECLIPSE

Monday, April 8th, 2024—the day a total solar eclipse was predicted to cast a band of darkness across North America, reaching clear from San Antonio, Texas, to Niagara Falls.

With an approximated totality of four-and-a-half minutes, people from all over the Midwest drove to hundreds of prime spots across several states, bringing lawn chairs and coolers in preparation to witness the literal "blotting of the sun".

As the last eclipse to cover Indiana was in the year 1205, my fiancé and I were ecstatic. We started planning the trip weeks before, researching each optimal spot within the 115 mile stretch that covered two-thirds of our Hoosier state. Vacation days were submitted, picnic plans were made, and we set our sights on what we thought to be the most optimal spot: *Shades State Park*, near the town of Crawfordsville, Indiana.

My fiancé, Sydney, is blind as a bat. She wears borderline bifocal glasses but absolutely hates wearing contacts. She hates the feeling of them against her eyelids. We did our research and looked into the best kind of special disposable eclipse glasses—which we learned were actually called *solar viewers*—as well as plenty of high SPF sunscreen to apply during our stay at Shades Park. Sydney has always been an over planner, writing notes and triple checking things *days* in advance before every occasion. Everything seemed cool, and with her obsessive habit of perfectly planning every outing, I didn't sweat the exciting day that was rapidly approaching.

That was, until the solar viewers came in the mail. They were chintzy little cardboard mass-produced pieces of garbage, but their crucial feature was there; the optical density 5 lenses, capable of blocking the eye-damaging radiation expected from the eclipse. But it wasn't their sharp paper arms or floppy integrity that posed the problem. The solar viewers were smaller than Sydney's glasses. Much smaller.

She groaned at the inconvenience, almost wanting to cancel the trip over the incompatibility. From what we could find online, they really only made one size. But as the days grew closer and the news headlines boasted of the "once in our lifetime experience", she relented, and decided she would make do with the contacts after all. If I would've known such a thing would cause something so horrible, I would've called the trip off myself. Looking back now, I'd give anything to go back and make us stay home.

On the morning of April 8th, Sydney and I packed up the car and embarked to our destination. Traffic was worse than we anticipated, the many construction zones packing everyone together into a boring, single lane route. After hours of stop-and-go traffic and every possible news iteration of the coming eclipse on the radio—most of them stressing repeatedly to **avoid looking directly into the sun's light**—we made it to Shades State Park, luckily snagging one of the last available parking spots. People from all over Indiana had made the trip out there, most of them hauling coolers and setting up blankets to claim their perfect spot to see the sky. We gathered our stuff and started scoping a place of our own, moving past the many occupied benches that looked towards a wide pond. Around the rim of the pond there was a wooden boardwalk that led to the park's hiking trails, with a decent sized shelf of grass on either side.

We decided that would be our perfect spot and promptly unfolded our canvas chairs. The rays above beat down over the pond aggressively, but there was a break in the neighboring trees that would give us a straight shot to the sun when we needed it. The only downside was the ground was riddled with mole tunnels, and it took us a moment to find solid ground for our chairs.

We lathered on sunscreen and collapsed contently into our chairs, grabbing cold drinks from the cooler and enjoying our nice view of the pond as the sun grew slowly more aggressive above. The pond was nice, fluttering with whiskered fish that hid amongst the murk in the deeper ends.

Parking overflowed shortly after, and groups passed by looking for their own spot, each of them muttering something like:

"You'll be ninety when this is supposed to happen again,"

"This won't happen for another seventy years!"

"I heard it wouldn't be for another hundred!"

Parasols, umbrella hats, and coolers on wheels. Some people started to pop beers like it was a celebration, others sprawled out on blankets with an open book while they patiently waited. I watched people through my sunglasses, occasionally putting the viewers underneath to look up and monitor the eclipse's progress. It was exciting watching the slow progression; one blinding light and one small sphere slowly converge.

We just sat and chilled for a while, munching on sandwiches and variety chip bags as we enjoyed being off work and away from home. Eclipse aside, it was nice to just get away and get from fresh air, especially out in nature.

Just as I was transfixed on the sky above, I heard Sydney cursing next to me. She was rifling through her backpack, checking every pocket in a panic.

"Syd, what's wrong?" I asked, but I had a gut feeling that I already knew.

"My contacts. I can't find the fucking contacts!" she exclaimed, moving on from the backpack and patting her shorts. Every pocket produced something—her phone, her keys, chapstick—but no contacts. In her frenzy, I felt the uncanny realization that not just the sky, but the world around us, was getting darker. Quickly.

"Are they in your purse? Do you want me to check the car?" I asked, trying to calm her down. I knew damn well that if she *had* brought them, she would've found them already. They were expensive, and even though she never wore them, she was paranoid of losing them.

"No, *fuck.* They would've been in the backpack, in the front pocket," she said, biting her lip in frustration. She looked around our canvas chairs, in the net pockets of the armrests, then underneath them. In a useless contribution, I flipped open the lid of the cooler and observed the bobbing canned drinks amongst the ice.

There was some commotion around us, and I was alarmed at the increasingly fleeting daylight. I felt the need to look at the sky again, but it felt shitty that I could safely look and she couldn't.

"I'll go check the car, I'll be right back," I said, already turning towards the parking lot.

"No, it's *fine.* Don't worry about it. I'll just deal with it. We're almost out of time. I didn't think it would get dark so quick."

"I'll be quick. We're supposed to have another thirty minutes or so. Just make sure you don't look up without the special ones," I said, already moving. I could hear her annoyance behind me, but I wanted to make an effort to check the car just in case. If she went, I had a feeling she would just give up and let me enjoy the moment while she sat it out. At least this way, if we both missed it, we could be disappointed together. Not to mention with the growing darkness, it would be easier for me to look around, anyway. Before I was out of earshot, Sydney sighed and called after me.

"Hurry up! I don't want *you* to miss it either."

I went to the parking lot as quickly as I could, preemptively getting out my phone to ready the flashlight once I opened the door. Maybe they had just fallen out at one of our gas station stops, or she had left her purse open at some point on the long drive over. I unlocked the car and immediately started digging, trying to ignore the other tourists *ooo's* and *aaaah's* as the darkness grew.

I went as quickly as I could. I checked under the seat first, then the center console, on top of the dash. Swinging wildly with the phone light, I checked the backseat, tossing around candy bar wrappers and empty pop bottles. Just as I was starting to give up hope, I wedged my hand in between the seat near the belt receptacle, and felt my fingers graze the undeniable shape of the figure-eight contact case.

They had fallen out after all.

I shoved my hand in and grabbed them, and quickly hopped out of the car, kicking the door shut behind me. I couldn't believe I had actually found them. I jogged down the gravel path, keeping eye contact with her in the fading light as I reached the boardwalk. I still had my sunglasses on so it was hard to see, but I could faintly make out her looking directly up, the solar viewers held against her thick framed glasses. There was something off with the way she was standing, though—totally motionless—like she was frozen in place. The people around her continued to cheer for the coming eclipse, but she didn't move at all. Nobody else seemed to notice either.

"Syd! I found them, they were stuck in the—" I tripped as soon as I rounded the boardwalk, my foot sinking into the network of mole tunnels. My ankle rolled and I hit the ground hard, the wind fleeing my lungs as felt flat on my stomach. I felt both my sunglasses and the chintzy viewers tumble away and splash into the pond.

When my vision settled, it was nearly pitch black. The critters in the forest around us had fallen silent, like the wildlife had fallen asleep. I could hear the dozens of people murmuring around us, each undoubtedly looking at the sky. It was happening so *fast*. There was supposed to be a schedule. We were supposed to still have time.

"Wow."

"Would you look at that."

"Marvelous isn't it? Once in a lifetime, I tell ya'."

I climbed to my feet and rushed to Sydney, who still hadn't moved. She maintained her same pose, the viewers placed over her glasses, but she didn't quite have them over her eyes. Through her squinted gaze, she was looking directly at the vanishing sun.

"Syd! I found them. It's probably too late, but—"

There was something wrong with her, and the closer I got, the clearer I could see. Her eyes were... blank. Like they had rolled into the back of her head. Tears trickled down her face, like she was weeping.

"Babe, are you okay? Babe?" clutching the contact case in my left hand, I reached out to her with the other to shake her. As soon as my fingers touched her arm, my vision blinked white.

The world was red. I could see everything now, like a crimson lens had been pulled over the sun. The first thing I noticed was the pond, and the lack of water in it. It was like it had dried up, leaving nothing but cracked earth in its wake.

"Babe?"

I heard a voice. *Sydney's.*

"What's going on?" I asked, unable to turn my head. I could feel her wrist in my hand, but I couldn't move. The only thing that seemed to obey was my eyes.

"I-I don't know. I tried to take a look with the glasses, but I think I looked directly into the sun. It was an accident, I didn't even think we were close to the eclipse yet. I thought I burned my eyes, but I saw this. Can you see this?" she said, and I could feel her trembling. It was like she wanted to gesture, wanted to move, but couldn't. She sounded terrified.

I tried to look to see her, but my body ignored me. I could just make out the frame of her body in the corner of my eye, a blurred figure that resembled the same pose she was in when I saw her.

"Yeah. I can see it," was all I could manage.

Above us, the sky was a neon orange that emitted a deep crimson glow. A singular black globe standing amongst the infinite floating hell. It looked like a black hole that was bleeding oil.

"I don't like this. How do we get out?"

The fear in her voice broke me. I tried to look away from the black hole in the sky, but it seemed to draw me in, like the cells in my body wanted to melt away.

"I don't know. We'll figure something out, I'm sure there's something going on—" I started.

"*Oh god.* Do you see that?"

Before I could ask what, I noticed it too. There was something in the middle of the dried-up pond. An egg, or a mushroom. Whatever it was, it was shifting. *Growing.*

"I see it."

"What is it? What do we do?" she asked. I could hear she was crying. I didn't understand. I didn't understand any of it. What the hell was all of this? Had we eaten something bad, had we been roofied somehow?

Nothing made sense.

"I don't know," I said, feeling miserably helpless. All I could feel was the contact lens container in my hand, her clammy wrist, and the increasingly cold sweat dripping down my back.

Wherever we were, it was humid, *hot,* but freezing. Ahead of us, the mysterious globe started to shift, jerking from side to side. A carapace-like shell cracked and split with a loud hiss of steam. An ectoplasmic goo writhed beneath. Even though I couldn't comprehend its existence, it felt malicious. Like we weren't supposed to be here.

"I'm sorry. I should've waited to look, I didn't think I'd even see anything," Sydney sobbed.

"It's ok, *it's ok.* We'll figure this out, maybe we're having some kind of reaction," I tried to reconcile, but I didn't even believe myself. I didn't know what the fuck was going on. It didn't make sense, it couldn't.

"Oh no, *oh god,*" Sydney shook in my grasp, but we still couldn't move. I wanted to pull her away and run for the car, but I couldn't move a single muscle. We were both frozen and helpless. I felt my heart race as I stared with her, my own cultivating fear taking my breath away.

Whatever it was that was in front of us, it was *blooming.* It was graceful at first, like a fresh flower. Then it was simply *wrong,* like a hotdog blowing up in a microwave. It was getting bigger. It was turning *inside out.*

"I don't want to die," Sydney said, but it felt like the emotion was fading from her voice. Above, the black sun continued to bleed, until it looked like the sphere itself was melting. The red glow intensified.

"We'll be ok," was all I could say. A lie, to us both.

The inside out bloom exploded violently, its innards fanning out like knives and teeth. They sprouted until they rooted themselves in the ground, and after several seconds passed, I realized what was happening.

A body was forming. Made completely of teeth.

The awkward shape bent heavily to one side, like a baby calf walking for the first time. It took a step, then two, before the waistline sprouted *more.* A torso. Shoulders with no head. Long, handless arms. It stood tall, at least a dozen feet. It only continued to dwarf and get taller with every step. It was so sharp, like a golem made of blades.

"Don't look at it Sydney, don't look!" I shouted, but my voice was muffled. Sydney wasn't shaking anymore. She felt relaxed, almost comfortable.

"It's beautiful, isn't it? Do you think it will hurt?" she asked, barely a whisper.

Above, the black sun exploded, scattering the light in a dance of shadows. My eyes watched like kaleidoscopes as it started to run, its hulking frame lumbering towards us.

Not us. Her.

"Sydney!"

———

I woke up to nothing. I thought it was death at first, until the fractured details started filtering in. Beeps. Muffled voices. The opening and closing of doors.

A hospital.

Once I spoke, I could sense the turmoil in the room. Nurses scattered to and fro, doctors were paged, vitals were checked. They asked questions for a time, but it took me a while to even understand them. My ears rang. It felt like my brain had been flash fried. I don't know how long it took for me to cooperate with them, for them to make any sense of me.

I kept asking for Sydney. I asked if she was alright. I asked where she was.

I couldn't see anything. There were bandages over my eyes, and my wrists were bound to my sides. I tried to get free of them or ask what happened. I demanded until I was screaming blindly, something that would usually end in them sedating me. In time, I accepted the silence, but every question yields either an awkward dismissal or an excuse.

I think it's been weeks. I'm not entirely sure. All I know is I'll be getting discharged soon. After the doctors, the nurses, my family, a man came to see me. He was patient, but cold and to the point. He asked me about April 8th, and what I was doing. Why I was there. If I wore glasses. What happened, in my own w ords.

I explained in detail, noting the events that happened, everything I could remember. Everything leading up to the exploding sun, and the being made of teeth. I asked him about the contacts, if they could at least give them to Sydney so she didn't lose them.

There was an awkward silence for a while before he finally cleared his throat.

And told me a very different story.

When questioned, bystanders reported I showed up and set up two chairs. I was nonchalant the whole time, even making small talk with someone that wasn't there. They said I *acted* like I showed up with someone. I had the disposable glasses, a cooler, a backpack. But it was only me. He said they asked every single person that went to the park that evening. People that had come from all over the state, well over a hundred. The ones that saw me all gave the same story.

They said once it started to get dark, I ran to my car to get something. When I got back, I took a nasty fall, and continued to talk to someone that wasn't there. Right before I looked up at the sky without the eye protection, like I was possessed.

That's when I started scratching out my eyes.

Apparently, several people tried to stop me, but I just screamed and clawed until there was nothing left but bone and bloody sockets. Paramedics arrived and found me inconsolable, ranting and raving about a black sun and teeth and a girl named Sydney. Eventually, they had to sedate me and escort me to the nearest hospital. The general consensus was I was mentally unwell or had stopped taking medication or something, and the irregular atmosphere of the eclipse caused me to have a manic episode.

I called bullshit throughout the whole story. I told the detective time and time again, about the black sun, the horrible monster, and how I thought it took Sydney. I told him I had proof, that I was carrying the contact lenses at the time it happened. They were *hers*.

The detective sighed again, and told me they had indeed found the case for the contact lens. I had brought it with me on the ambulance ride over, squeezing it so hard until it tore my skin and nearly shattered. They inspected it thoroughly, and to their surprise, there *were* contact lenses in there. But the prescription didn't belong to anybody, not me, or anyone by the name of Sydney.

Furthermore, they couldn't find any record of her at all. As if she had never existed in the first place.

THE PACKAGE

As the mailbox came into view, I pulled onto the shoulder. I put it in park and stared up at the driveway, an uneven set of ruts that disappeared into the dance of willows that struggled against the storm. Through the whipping vines I could see the faint glow, a sign that someone was home, weathering the hell that was this storm.

I watched for a time, listening to the rain batter the windshield through the repetitive squeal of wipers. My heart raced under the film of it all. The wind tearing through the trees, the bright flash of lightning, the heavy rumble in the sky. The house, lurking in the darkness.

On the passenger seat was the package, along with the manilla envelope. I picked up the envelope and ran my thumbs over it. I had flipped through them a hundred times over the past two weeks, and still I found myself opening it. I didn't look long. The toothy smile, the soft face, the innocent eyes. Just seeing the photographs made me anxious.

I set the envelope down and ran a hand over the box. Light brown cardboard, sealed with packing tape, an address crudely written in sharpie. It would make it through the storm if I moved fast enough.

I killed the engine and watched the storm swallow the road ahead. I pocketed the keys and tucked the envelope under the cab's arm rest. In the backseat was a gym bag, already open and filled with miscellaneous things. I turned on the dome light and reached back, my hand searching the contents until my fingers found what I was looking for. Digging through blindly, my eyes flicked between the oncoming road and the desolate driveway, to the faint glow in the distance.

They were home. This was my chance.

One by one, I withdrew the items from the bag, holding them to the light to see. A beige ball cap. A reflective poncho. A clipboard with a newspaper cutout attached to it. Satisfied, I tucked the duffel bag behind the seat and moved on to the glovebox. I popped it open and lifted the registration and collection of napkins, to the two more important items underneath. A .38 snub-nose revolver, and a half pint of whiskey. Both items glared back coldly, and I wondered for a moment if this time I could go without.

Go big or go home.

I ejected the cylinder and counted the rounds before tucking it into the back of my waistband. My gaze in the rearview mirror watched as I tilted the bottle to my lips. The burn was harsh, but soothing. Two drinks, almost half of it. Probably too much. I tossed the bottle back and slapped the glove box shut, the 'click' of the dome light leaving me in a dull, surreal barrage of rain. I sat there for a moment, listening to the storm as I braced myself for what was to come.

I gathered up the clipboard and package and threw open the door.

The rain was coming down in sheets. The ball cap helped a little, but once the wind picked up, I had to hold on to it so it didn't blow away. With one hand on the bill and the other ushering my items under the poncho, I crossed the street and ascended the slippery hill of a driveway. Puddles splashed and the mud squelched, and as I made my way to the top, I squinted through the rain at the house in the distance. Parked sloppily in the gravel drive was a red sedan, one with a familiar license plate.

I moved quickly, the warmth of the whiskey pushing me through the storm. I held the package close, the events of recent days playing through my mind as I climbed the steps. Underneath the poncho, I felt the reminding weight of the revolver. By the time I stood in front of the door, I was thoroughly soaked. I took a deep breath and thought of the words I had recited dozens of times. I raised my fist to the door.

Three hard knocks.

"U.S. Postal Service!" I shouted against the rain.

Inside the house, someone cursed and stirred. Male. Gruff. "What the hell?"

I heard the groan of a recliner, and the heavy footsteps moving toward the door. I took a second to peek through the windows, just long enough to get a feel. A television's glow on an empty couch. A pizza box left open. A little paper plate, with two slices untouched. The absence of light in the rooms beyond.

On the other side of the door, several locks were disengaged. An upper latch, a deadbolt, the knob. The door pulled open just enough for a chain lock to snap taut, followed by an angry glare.

"What do you want?" the glaring man had a shaved head, multiple face tattoos, with sunken eyes. After he locked eyes with me, he looked past me to see if I was with anyone.

"U.S. Postal Servi—"

"I'm not expecting a package, get lost."

He went to slam the door, and I stopped it with my foot, clearing my throat.

"Sir, if you choose to refuse the package, I'll have to file it as 'return to sender'. I'll make note that this specific address chose not to sign for it. Is there a reason why you're refusing the package?"

"What?" he asked, annoyed.

"This is, uh," I paused, feigning a look at the clipboard "Twelve hundred East, Five-hundred South, right?"

He paused and looked me up and down before looking past me.

"Yeah?" he said impatiently.

"Look, can you at least open the door and look at this thing, to verify it's a mistake? I'm gettin' soaked out here," I urged, holding the box close.

"Just leave it on the doorstep and get out of here," he said.

"It has to be signed for," I reminded. "If this is a bad time, I can try again tomorrow. I'll just make a note here and leave you to it." I raised the clipboard, and he groaned.

"*Fine.* You can come in, but only for a second."

"Of course, I appreciate—"

He shut the door hard and cut me off, and I heard the rattle of the chain lock as he removed it. The door opened a second later, revealing a wiry man in jeans and a dirty wife-beater. He stood with his chest puffed out for a moment, making me wait awkwardly before motioning to come inside. I shook the loose rainwater off me and ducked in, looking around the room as quickly and discreetly as I could. He pushed the door shut behind me.

"Thanks. Some weather, huh? It's freezing out there," I said, taking note of the surroundings. The television was on, an old program playing of a woman cheerily sewing dolls together. Ahead of it was the coffee table and the remnants of a pizza dinner that nobody ate. A little plate with no bites taken, and a big plate that looked like the food had just been pulled apart and played with. All blanketed in an aroma of rotting garbage, my guess was from the various overfilled bags near the island in the kitchen—

"I didn't see you pull in. Where's your truck?" he asked blankly, scratching his head. He was built like a construction worker, his body covered in crude tattoos and scars. I thought of the whiskey, and wished I drank more of it.

"Oh? I'm surprised you didn't see me struggling out there. Truck couldn't make it up the drive. Too muddy. Believe it or not, the things are only rear-wheel drive," I chuckled, drumming my fingers on the box. My hands were clammy against the damp cardboard.

"Pizza guy made it just fine," he grumbled. I felt a chill on my neck.

"Right. I'm afraid we got a pretty big haul in the back. With Christmas coming up, and all," I held the clipboard out to him, "well, if you wouldn't mind signing, I'll be on my way."

He took it hesitantly, his eyes locked onto mine for a time before falling to the clipboard. I took a deep breath and tried not to straighten as I watched his expression from aggravated to confused. His eyes narrowed, then widened.

"What—just *what the fuck is this supposed to be?*" he growled, showing me the clipboard. I didn't look at it. His other hand curled into a fist.

I showed him the box, the scribbling in the corner with a black marker.

"This *is* the correct address, is it not?" I kept my cool.

He was flustered, rapidly unwinding. Even still, he read the box, sensing the importance of it.

His eyes went wild as he read it to himself, and I tried not to flinch against the incoming outburst.

"Who the fuck are you, huh?! Who sent you?" he spat, throwing the clipboard at me.

"If you can just verify that the address is correct, I can—"

"Who are you?!" He was on me in an instant. Heavy hands grabbed fistfuls of the poncho and my clothes alike. He slammed me into the refrigerator so hard it rocked back and forth. The clipboard and package tumbled to the floor.

"U.S. Postal—"

"*Bullshit.* What the fuck are you doing here, how'd you find me?" His hands tore the fabric, nearly lifting me off the ground. He side eyed the windows, to the rain battering the empty driveway. Nothing but the red sedan, and a whole lot of mud

"That wouldn't happen to be your car 91 Sentra out there, would it? Anybody else home?" I asked plainly, dropping the act. His face went slack.

"I'll kill you,"

I grit my teeth and hoped for a punch. I got the island instead. The countertop slammed into my hip as I tried to resist, my shoes squeaking against the floor and I was tossed over it. I rolled to the other side in a hail of garbage and utensils, landing hard on my shoulder. As I tried to get to my feet, I heard him coming around, stomping through the debris as he seethed. It wasn't enough.

"It was only a matter of time. If not me, someone else," I said, just in time for him to rush me again. He was stronger but clumsy, thrashing out like a child would in a tantrum. I saw the punch coming, his weight behind it. The most prominent knuckle crashed into my cheek, and I felt the bloody swirl of the molar knocking loose. Through the scuffle, I heard it bounce off the tile

.

"You made a mistake coming here. Should've just left me alone!" He barked, shoving me into the counter. I tried to worm out of his grasp, the hat falling and poncho tearing as he shoved me against the kitchen sink. I watched the room blur in the scuffle as the blows rained down. A punch in the gut, a knee in the side, an elbow in the ribs. His hands clamped around my throat and my back bent painfully into the sink, the overflow of dishes collapsing against me. Forks and spoons skittered away, and a glass shattered against the tile.

His eyes were wild, his teeth bared. I forced my chin down to try and halt the asphyxiation, and he responded with a punch to the eye. Feeling my brow swell and welt under the impact of his knuckles, I felt an immediate clarity through the haze of violence. As he reared back for another punch, I grabbed him by the shoulders and drove my knee between his legs.

"Goddamn you," he groaned as he hunched over, his grip weakening. As I tried to shove him off and move away, he grabbed a fistful of hair and yanked me away from the sink, throwing me towards the living room. A stool bounced off my shin and I met the carpet face first next to the recliner.

Behind me, the man groaned. I heard the angry toss of the counter's contents, followed by the metallic ring from a knife block.

"I'll gut you before you can take her away!" he shouted, his feet kicking through debris. I heard him kick one of the trash bags in frustration, the contents spilling out by my feet.

Underneath the poncho, my hand gripped the revolver. I rolled over, aimed the gun with both hands, and fired.

Two shots, center mass.

My ears rang as the bullets punched into him, and two dark spots overtook the stains on his wife-beater. The man stumbled back in surprise, falling into a heap against the island, the knife held close as he pawed at the wounds. He rambled incoherently, a string of starting sentences that faded quickly.

The gun shook in my hands, and my trigger finger itched to give him one more. With a final hateful look, the man expired, his face freezing into a permanent mask of disdain. Even after his head drooped and his arms went limp, I kept the gun on him. My chest heaved and my heart raced. I stood there for a time in the glow of the television, watching the body as my ears rang. The sweat on my forehead chilled, and I felt the steady trickle of rainwater down my back.

I nudged him with my foot. Nothing. I looked down the hall, to the darkness of the rest of the house. Nobody came running; no frantic spouse, no panicked children, no riled dog.

Nothing.

I deflated for a moment, wiping my brow, and feeling the throb of where I had been struck. As my nerves calmed, I looked at the room around me, seeing what I could make work. I wouldn't have much time. I dug into my pocket and pulled a pair of latex gloves, feeling anxious as the prophylactic drug across my skin.

I went into the kitchen and navigated the debris from the scuffle. Paper plates, silverware, and broken glass had been strewn everywhere, most of what had been collected on the island went I went over it. I positioned each step gingerly, trying to keep my footing on the trash specifically as I located what I had lost.

I found the ball cap on the floor near the stove. I picked it up and shook the glass from it before moving on. The clipboard and the package were on the floor where he had first charged me. I grabbed them both and set them on the island. Attached to the clipboard was a newspaper article, still legible despite the damage the rain had done to it. I removed it and folded it up before pocketing it.

Next I moved onto the package. The box was soaked, the packing tape already starting to peel against the wet container. It opened easily. I took the item from within and placed it next to the clipboard, before crumpling the box as much as I could.

With the clipboard and crumpled box in hand, I stepped over the dead man and moved to one of the full trash bags near the island, to one that hadn't been knocked over. The bag had been barely tied, and came undone easily enough. It opened with a buzz of flies. I dug through the trash gently, pushing what I could to one side to create an alcove in the contents. Once I was satisfied, I took off the poncho.

I wrapped the clipboard, ballcap, and crumpled box in a little wad, and stuffed it into the garbage as deep as I could get it, before covering it up and re-tying it. After positioning it as it was before I touched it, I stepped back and observed the room.

The kitchen was a disaster. The corpse was now bleeding from the mouth, a slow drool that blended into the blooms on his stomach. Behind me, the sewing program droned on, and the storm continued to rage outside, like nothing had ever happened.

I grabbed the item from the package and started down the hall. The rest of the house was dark, and I flipped on the lights as I went. There were four doors in the hall, so I started with the closest.

The first was a bathroom and had nothing of interest. A small sink and toilet, accompanied by a bathtub and shower. No paraphernalia, no signs of struggle or violence. I moved on, shutting the light off behind me.

The second was a linen closet, one that hadn't been used for anything except junk storage. Dated boxes of "As seen on TV" products, an ironing board, some hangers. Nothing of value, no hiding dark secrets.

The next room, I assumed, was the bedroom for the dead man. A single yellowed mattress and box spring on the floor, one pillow, one blanket. An old dresser, a small closet. There were numerous sets of dumbbells and workout equipment on the floor. The garbage buildup was present in the room as well, but was mostly restricted to empty beer cans and takeout containers. I minded the trash and checked the dresser drawers; the ones that weren't empty contained only a stray pair of odd clothing, like a single sock, or long johns.

The closet held the most interest, but nothing really incriminating. Old flannels hung on wooden hangers. A used fish tank complete with a heating unit and bubble wand. A hunting rifle from the 90's, leaning in the corner. Several old tins housing sewing utensils and thread. I closed the closet and ignored my rising heart rate. I dabbed my brow with my sleeve and left the bedroom, shutting off the light and closing the door behind me.

Looking at the last door at the end of the hall, I felt a familiar sickening churn in my stomach. The door was just as old and dated as the rest in the house, but there was one crucial detail that made me nauseous.

An after-market padlock that kept it locked from the outside.

I felt an encroaching darkness at the sight of it, an eerie validation of my presence. The padlock was cheap but effective nonetheless, and the longer I looked at it, the more I tried not to panic. Across the face of the lock was the name of a generic brand: *Secur-Lock.*

I would need a key.

I had already tossed the dresser and closet, as well as any other obvious location for such a thing. I didn't have to mull it over long before I found myself looking in the direction of the island down the hall.

To the dead man in the kitchen.

Kneeling in front of his corpse was far from pleasant. The stillness of his body, the chill of his apparent departure, the slow drool from his lips. I dug into his pockets gently, trying not to disturb his natural point of decomposition.

His right-hand pocket was empty, save for some loose change. In his left, I found a string of keys. Among the rings were several keys; one to the front door—knob and deadbolt, one to the Sentra, a cheap toolbox key, and a small nickel-plated key. Looking over them all, I noticed the nickel-plated was decorated in the same *SecurLock* logo. I pulled it from the ring and returned the others to his pocket before moving on.

I left the dead man and moved back to the door at the end of the hall. I inserted the key to the padlock and twisted, feeling a rush of anxiety as it popped open. The knob turned, and I opened the door, revealing an old, dark wooden staircase.

And a stench of heavy, decrepit rot.

I descended the stairs slowly, drawing the pistol in my off hand while the other clutched the item from the package. Each step was agonizing and deliberate, like I was walking into hell. The steps creaked and the darkness swallowed me as I went in, but through the void, I could see a sign of light.

In the middle of the floor was a television, playing the same program from the living room. A cheery woman sewing the seams of dolls, the glow of the tube lighting the floor in front of it.

Laying on the floor of the basement, was a little girl. Her wrists were bound with zip-ties, her dress dirty and stained. The air was thick with the stench of death.

When I reached the landing, she stirred. A weak whimper escaped her lips, and she barely had the strength to lift her head. Even in the desolate dark, I could recognize her.

I took off the latex gloves, dug out my phone, and dialed three numbers with a shaking thumb. I listened to the dial tone in the dark, my eyes slowly adjusting to the rest of the basement, to the *things* lining the walls.

When the operator picked up, the sound of my voice filled the room.

"This is Private Investigator Don Spencer. I'm at Twelve Hundred East, Five-Hundred North, just outside Dyer Falls. I need an ambulance immediately. There's been shots fired, and there's a child that needs immediate medical assistance. My car is on the shoulder near the driveway. We'll be on the porch waiting for you."

Once the operator assured me help was on the way, I hung up.

"Hello? Is someone there?" the girl asked weakly, squinting through the dark.

I moved toward the girl slowly, trying not to scare her. I held out the item from the package, close enough so she could see it. As her eyes adjusted, I looked at the walls cautiously, a cold sweat chilling on my neck.

She looked at the little stuffed polar bear, its fur catching the light.

"Hello Vanessa. My name is Don, I'm a friend of your parents. They sent me here to find you. It's safe now. Would you mind coming with me, so we can get you out of here? Let's get you home."

I held the bear out, hoping to keep her eyes on it. To keep her eyes off everything else in the basement. I could only faintly make them out. Humanoid figures with crude stitching and canvas for skin. Their beady glass eyes in the TV's glow. Their heads cocked, positioned on the girl in front of me. Some of them were starting to move.

She looked at the bear and started to cry.

"I want to go home. I don't want to be here anymore."

I gave her the bear, and while she held it, I cut the zip-ties with a pocketknife. I instructed her to keep her eyes on it, and she nodded compliantly, nestling against me while I picked her up. I carried her up the stairs and out of the basement, away from the nightmares that no longer felt the need to hide in the shadows. I could hear their little steps, the pitter patter of shambling horrors. When I made it to the top of the steps, I slammed the door behind me—just in time to see that the dolls had nearly closed the distance between us. Their eyes were dead and menacing, each rotten globe carrying a deep rage directed at me. I fumbled the lock until it was locked once more and moved away from the basement entrance quickly.

By the time I carried her down the hall, I could hear the sirens coming. I ushered her past the dead man in the kitchen and out onto the porch, away from the destruction of the house and the ungodly things within it. The storm had settled by then, a light drizzle pattering the mud by the time the first cruiser came into view. In the red and blue glow, I sat on the porch with her and raised a hand passively as they got out of the car.

After missing for two weeks, the following morning, Vanessa Williams was reunited with her parents. As they rejoiced, I gave my statement.

I explained I was a Private Investigator, and had been hired by the William's to find more information regarding their daughter's disappearance. While there wasn't much information at the time of Vanessa's abduction, I had taken upon myself to re-question everyone in the neighborhood, specifically the residents living on the same block as the William's. Most of the evidence gathered was either inconclusive or irrelevant to the crime, however there were two residents claiming to have seen a specific "red sedan" driving around the area at the same time the abduction had taken place.

I did some routine door-to-door questioning, nothing too invasive. There had been a long list of missing persons in the town, so the locals were pretty forthcoming with information. Stopping by many houses outside city limits, mostly looking for a red car in the driveway, rumored abnormal behavior, stuff like that. When I couldn't find anything in town, I started pushing outside city limits, county-line roads and the like.

I stopped at a house on a long list on a road outside of town. The owner happened to have a 91 Nissan Sentra in the driveway. I knocked professionally and inquired about asking some questions, to which they obliged. Owner of the house let me in without any trouble. Everything was going well until I heard shouting coming from the basement. The owner got angry and started attacking me, unprovoked. Like a switch had been flipped. I tried to talk them down, but ended up having to pull my concealed-carry firearm, and shot them twice. I was not happy I had to do it, but they forced my hand. I went into the basement to follow up on the screaming to see if there was someone in danger, and found a girl tied up in the basement.

I called for medical assistance immediately.

They never found my newspaper clipping with the headline of Vanessa's disappearance. Or the cardboard box, with Vanessa's address I had written on myself. Or the disguise I used, my means to get in. It all got shoveled with the rest of the house trash, never to be found again.

Following my report, Dyer Falls P.D. scoured the entire house. What first looked to be a simple child-abduction case turned into an investigation of a house of horrors. "The Doll House", they would come to name it. It's unfortunate to say that Vanessa Willaims was not just the victim of a spontaneous abduction, but a notch on a long list of disturbing acts tucked within the outskirts of Dyer Falls. While on the surface, the house just looked lazily unkempt and unorganized, the basement of the property would tell a different story.

The basement in which Vanessa was kept also served as a burial ground for more than twenty other young girls (all ranging from ages 6-12). Jakob Hamm, the now deceased owner of the property, has been tied to the killings of multiple young girls. Each seemed to have been kept and starved for long periods of time, before ultimately killed by strangulation. The bodies were then covered, or "sewn" as the media has taken to calling it, by stitching cloth faces and dresses over the corpses postmortem.

I kept specifics of my eye-witness account out of my report, for obvious reasons. I know it would haunt my dreams for years to come, but there was no point in complicating things, particularly my report and my career to follow. Some secrets are best left unsaid.

A recent dig into Hamm's files has shown that he has been admitted for psychiatric evaluation several times in the past—four times since his mother's passing in adolescent years, and two after his deployment to Afghanistan through the U.S. Army, since getting dishonorably discharged for things <redacted> in his time in the field. It is unclear exactly as to what drove Hamm's to conduct such atrocities, but it is sure that the events will hang as a stain above Dyer Falls's history as a town and shake the people for years to come.

Jakob was the last living member of the Hamm Family, since the passing of his mother, Amelia Hamm.

A woman once known for her love of dolls, and the timeless ideals they represent.

THE THING ON THE BALCONY

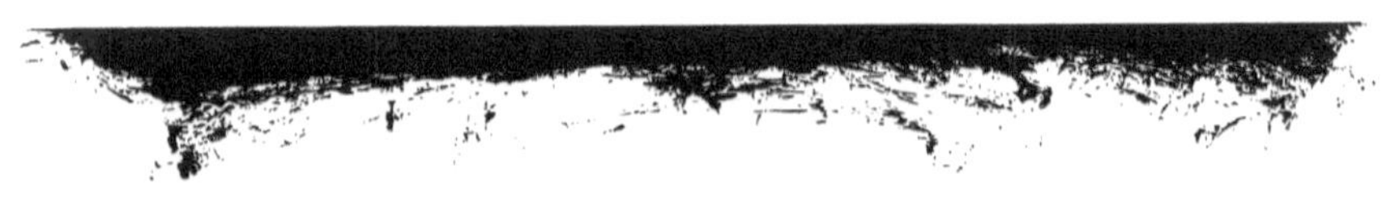

The pizza box was too big to fit in the fridge. I thought of this when I woke up, a little harmless thought as I finished the last of the water on the nightstand.

The water was good, really good, but it wasn't enough. I finished the water and decided to get up for more, and in doing so, I thought of the obnoxious pizza box still sitting on the stove.

I got more water, took it back to the bedroom. Son was sleeping on the wife's side of the bed, and I vaguely recalled them switching during the night. He took her side because he thought he saw a monster. She took his room to get away from my snoring. More harmless thoughts. I sauntered over to the collection of water glasses on the nightstand and placed tonight's refill.

On the stove sat the pizza box. I opened it quietly like a thief in the night. Grabbed a piece, sausage. Just a quick piece, then back to bed, a little bit more water, back to sleep.

First bite—all the fucking toppings come off. A bare, sauce-soaked, not-as-tantalizing piece of crust shining in the soft light of the stove's range hood. Panic, paper towel. Try to salvage it, place the crust on the counter, wipe my mouth with the paper towel, walk it off.

I saw it then, on the balcony.

I froze, watching it, the paper towel still held mid-smear on my mustache. It had seen me, too. And it was watching back.

We had left the blinds open, pulled just enough to the side to see out. They've been remodeling the balconies, but there were enough planks to hold something outside the glass, seven feet tall. Was it eight? As I watched it, I couldn't recall if I had checked the time.

I didn't want to chance a look. My phone was in the bedroom, near the collection of water glasses. If I had it, I could call the police.

But I'd have to look away from it.

It was just standing there, standing awkwardly like it had been caught in the act. And I was reminded of how long it had been since we used the slider, *how long it's been since we knew it was locked.*

I thought of him, sleeping next to the still warm spot I left behind. I thought of her, off in the other room to get away from the snoring.

I could scream.

But then what? Then we'd all just be fuckin' scared.

I went to the balcony, moving slow, lowering the paper towel as I crossed the living room. Getting the details of it the closer I got—or the lack thereof.

Long, spindly fucking arms. A hunched back. A dead hang of thin hair. It's almost December—where were its clothes? Why my balcony?

It seemed happy to see me. Like this was a pleasant surprise. I felt the spike in my blood pressure, the collecting sweat in my armpits. A paper towel instead of a phone, *or a bat.* And I stood there, looking at it.

Too scared to see if it was locked, too worried to check. Standing in the ringing, suffocating silence of the living room, I asked the only thing I could think of.

"What do you want?"

I couldn't actually hear my voice when it spoke, but it understood. Its face started to droop, a sag of skin and a slow look that drifted to the left—to my son's room. Where she slept in the child's bunk bed, to get away from the snoring.

A slow look that listed lazily back to me—then past me—to where my bedroom would be. To the eight-year-old sprawled on her side of the bed.

Looking into its eyes, I felt my lip tremble. Not like this.

Looking into its eyes, I mouth the word.

No.

It takes a deep breath and leans against the outer frame of the slider. It gets worse the longer I look. It's a fucking nightmare. It has to be a dream. Its lungs inflate and its chest puffs out, and its skin hangs off its fucking bones. It's trying to intimidate me. It opens its mouth to talk—it makes no sound—but I understand what it's trying to say.

The words chill my bones.

I have all night.

I think of her in his room, I think of him on her side of the bed. Paper towel squeezed in my hand, a reminder that I didn't take a leak when I got more water.

So do I.

The response amuses it, and it shrugs. We'll see, it says. It moves, and I panic and think it's going to try and come in. I don't think I could stop it. Its unnatural human form twists as it settles in, its limbs folding unnaturally to sit like a dog—*or a horse.*

It mocks me. I sit on the carpet and wait, trying to project this is no big deal. Trying to shield the fact that I'm terrified. It looks like it's freezing outside, the way it shivers. Thin skin on pointy bones, a face that won't stop sagging. We're supposed to get snow soon. It's freezing in the living room. I'm in my boxers. Goosebumps crawl over my skin.

We stare at each other. I don't know if there's rules. I don't know if I can look away, or if I can check if it's locked or not. I don't think I can stop it.

What happens if I fall asleep, or *they wake up.*

I sit. I watch it, it watches me. The dark night ticks away. I don't know when it started, I don't know when it's going to end.

The longer I look, the worse it gets. Sometimes it pretends to fall asleep. *It's fucking with me.* The worst part, the worst part of all…

Sometimes the mold slips. Whatever's holding it, whatever the illusion is that serves as its existence. Like a twitch. As if its normal form wasn't bad enough.

Whatever's underneath. Sometimes it's a flash of teeth and a spread of gore—like an aftermath of a hit and run. Sometimes it's up against the glass, its body flattening, its eyes staring hard at me, trying to scare me.

Sometimes it's a girl, its mouth hanging open in a soundless scream.

Sometimes there are no eyes at all.

I sit and watch. Terrified to look away. Terrified it'll get impatient. The hours tick away, and behind it, the sun starts to break over the trees. Before the rays can touch its skin, it sighs deliberately.

It's out of time. A single nod serves as my congratulations, and as it looks to her in his room, and him in my bed, its final words haunt me.

You got lucky this time.

It slips away in an instant, its limbs taking it back to woods. Back to whatever hell it came from.

My body aches and I'm soaked in sweat. I wait until the sun is shining, the only way I'll think I'm safe. When I'm ready, I get up and check the slider.

It wasn't locked.

Once I fix that, I check the front door. Deadbolt and knob were both turned—but it doesn't make me feel better. I don't think I'll ever feel better again.

In my hand is the paper towel, nearly perished under my squeezed grip. On the counter is a cold piece of bare pizza, the exposed sauce reminding me of the monster. I put them both in the trash.

I creep to his room and find her sleeping peacefully. I creep back to mine and find him sprawled on my side. The water on the nightstand chills as I down the glass in one go. I place the empty next to the others, and I slowly lie down next to him, hoping I don't wake him. Hoping I don't hear anything aside from his soft little snores.

I listen to the snores and wonder if it's even possible to go back to sleep. If I'll ever sleep again.

THE EXTENSION CORD HOUSE

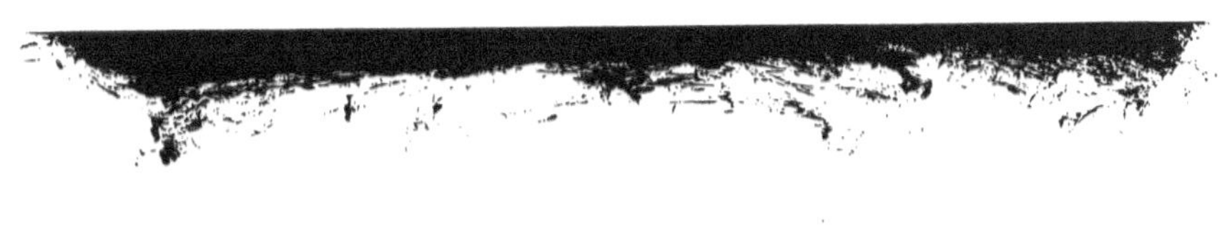

T he house stood amongst the trees like an open sore, a condemned heap of lumber and tattered shingles that was dwarfed by the forest surrounding it. The structure begged to be demolished, and the wildlife looked ready to reclaim it at a moment's notice. The longer I looked at it, the more I wondered if I was at the wrong address.

My watch beeped and I lowered the binoculars, feeling the chilly air nip at the back of my neck. It had just turned ten o'clock, but lying in the weeds, it felt like three in the morning. The moon couldn't seem to get a word in through the clouds, and the house itself seemed to radiate its own perpetual darkness. Even from across the street, the house felt *wrong*.

I got off my stomach and crouched in the grass, chewing my lip. My gut urged me to go home, and I thought of my car, parked on the agricultural road about a hundred yards away. I could just leave and forget about this place, forget it even existed. Just the thought of leaving made me feel guilty, and I couldn't help but dig my phone out of my pocket. I thought of Teddy, and I started to sweat.

I read the text again, for the thousandth time.

-Heading there now, sure you haven't changed your mind?-

Teddy was my younger brother. We didn't have the best childhood growing up—between our father being in and out of prison and our mother working double shifts, we were left to our own devices the majority of the time. It was something that made us stray from the path of normal blue-collar children. With my mother struggling to make ends meet and the continuous lack of money, it was easy to pick us out from the other kids at school, something that would eventually get us into constant trouble in years of bullying and being outcasts. Despite the hardship, Teddy and I found ways to ease our path through a life where money had the final say.

We started taking it whenever we could.

It started small, and innocently if I might add. A couple bucks here and there from other students, enough to afford things we didn't have, like laundry, soap or deodorant. With enough practice, we learned to lift wallets and purses with ease. We preyed on other students at our high school for whatever cash their parents sent them with, be it book rental fees or lunch money.

It wasn't personal, it was just there. And the worst part of it all, the money came easy.

We always distanced ourselves from the owners of the money we took, and we only attempted if we were sure we could get it without there being an altercation. We didn't want to be anywhere near them when they realized it was gone, either. In the end, I think it helped with our guilt. For all we knew, they assumed they lost it.

When we got older and out of school, we started casing places together. *Planning.* Trying to be better. Pickpocketing on the street was tough, and the pay didn't justify the risk. We hit our first house before we were twenty, spent weeks making sure they wouldn't be home. At first, the few hundred bucks in cash didn't seem worth it, but the yield from pawning trinkets ended up being the real prize. Engagement rings, heirloom watches, coin collections. The investment of scoping houses and scouring them would triple, sometimes quadruple a day of pulling wallets. Each score would provide enough to catch everything up and buy necessities, even allow a few weeks of downtime.

As the years passed we honed our craft, planning each job patiently, methodically. Countless hours practicing lockpicking on dummy locks and researching home surveillance. Memorizing mail routes, garbage pickup.

The best houses to hit were those who went out on the town for the night. Whether it be a club, or a casino.

We were pretty damn good at it, too. Enough to make a living off of it, easily. We would spend two weeks planning and hit the house on the weekend. Everything seemed to be going well, almost *foolproof,* until the last house we hit together. Teddy was getting impatient. Cocky. Swore only one week of planning would be enough, that we were taking too much time. I reluctantly agreed, my gut feeling pushed away by the thought of the extra money.

We cased a place outside of town and waited for a Friday night. Watching from the field across the street, we observed as a couple left and locked the door behind them, all dressed up for a night out. They got in the only car in the driveway and drove away, the house barely lit with some of the kitchen lights on. Nobody else looked to be inside. The coast looked clear.

Teddy stood watch while I picked the lock, and when we got in, we went straight to the bedroom. We tossed the drawers and moved on to the closet like we usually did, but something wasn't right. The lights started to come on in the house, followed by the scuffs of little feet on the carpet.

Standing in the doorway was a preteen girl, and three little kids, each had to be under ten years old. Turns out the babysitter and the couple's children had been hanging out in the basement, watching movies. Together we all froze, the children terrified and crying as they looked at the two scary men in ski-masks, their eyes falling to the crowbars in our hands. Teddy was the first to move, raising his crowbar in an attempt to scare them off. The kids started to scream, and I told Teddy to back off, deciding it was best to just call it a bust and walk away.

We had to jump through the window and make a run for it, and we got away clean, but there was something about that night that put me off the whole thing. The look in their eyes when they caught us, and the uncertainty I felt when Teddy walked toward them.

I didn't want to do it anymore. Despite Teddy's frustration, I went clean, got a job stocking goods at a local store, earning an actual check while I sat on my nest egg. Teddy tried to do the same, but proved unable to adjust to a normal life where money had to be earned instead of taken. I tried to get him on the right track, and he tried to fight me every step of the way. In the end, we parted ways, and he went back to casing places alone while I spent my nights stocking shelves and trying to blend in as a normal person.

As the months passed, I started to enjoy my new attempt at life. I even met a girl at the store I was working at, and we started seeing each other. We didn't have a lot of money, and I was slowly bleeding my nest egg going on dates and buying things for my apartment. The urge to do another job would return, but each time I would think of the look of terror on the faces of those kids, and it would melt away.

Even last week, when I got a text from Teddy. Another attempt to get me back in, something he would do every couple weeks, despite our falling out. He had been doing jobs on his own for a while now, focusing on houses out in the country. Said he had found one almost completely surrounded by trees, one that nearly looked abandoned. There were rumors a hoarder had lived there. He talked a good game and even sent me the address. I knew he wanted me back because we worked better as a team. The thought was tantalizing, imagining finding a nice necklace or earrings, something I couldn't afford with my wage job. Aside from the money, I missed the bond we shared when we worked together. I missed *him*. The act of no longer doing the jobs and trying to be clean cut felt like

I was missing a limb. Despite the lure to join him, I refused. I couldn't get the image of the children from the last job out of my head.

Three days ago, he sent me another text.

-Heading there now, sure you haven't changed your mind?-

I refused again and wished him well, and as he went off to make more than three of my checks put together, I went on a date instead.

When I got back home, I texted him to see how it went, and he didn't respond. He didn't answer my calls, either. Even though we weren't working together anymore, he still always answered his phone. The next day, I went to his apartment and found he wasn't home. His car wasn't there, either.

I checked public records to see if he had gotten arrested. When that turned nothing up, I started to worry. I looked up the address and placed an anonymous phone call through wifi-calling at the local library. They performed a wellness check, and said, "not only was there no one there, it looked like the place was going to cave in at any second." They assumed I had given them the wrong address.

Another day passed. Another day of calling, stopping by his apartment, checking everywhere he would've normally been. It was like he had just vanished out of thin air. The only lead I had was the house.

This house.

I looked at the text for a little bit longer before tucking my phone away. I climbed onto my knees and looked through the binoculars again, panning them over the porch, the windows, the driveway. It really did look like it was going to collapse at any second.

I checked both sides of the street and saw the same abyssal darkness for as far as I could see. There wasn't a car coming for miles in either direction. I walked quickly up the driveway, my backpack feeling oddly comforting on my shoulders. I had brought everything I would need to get into the house; my worn set of lockpicks, a flashlight, and my crowbar. I had dressed dark and in layers to fight against the chill, but my blood was running hot at the thought that something had happened to Teddy.

I walked quickly, repeatedly scanning between the door and the windows and making sure there wasn't any movement. The house already looked like it would be painless to get into. No CCTV, no automatic porchlight, no key code lock, no barking dog. This would've been easy money, if the place didn't look like it had been abandoned for twenty years.

The porch steps creaked under my feet as I climbed them, preemptively readying my picks by the time I hit the door. I worked quickly, inserting the tensioner and jimmying the pick until the plug turned. I glanced behind me to make sure nobody was there and turned the knob. The knob turned freely but the door didn't budge. Not like it was being held by a deadbolt, like it wasn't moving *at all*. Midway through the door was a mail slot, and I lifted the cover to peek in.

There was nothing but a dusty gloom. No lighting, whatsoever.

I pocketed the picks and pulled the little crowbar from my bag, wedging the tip in between the door and the frame around it. The wood splintered, but the door remained solidly in place—I would be here all day and all I would get was a mess.

Crowbar in hand, I left the porch and circled around the house, looking through the windows as I worked my way to the back. The windows were covered in a film of dust and dirt, and I could barely see inside. I decided I would find a way in through the back, away from the view of the road.

The lawn was erratically overgrown, tufts of weeds protruding up to waist height that nearly made me trip every other step. The dark outside seemed to suffocate, and between the lack of visibility and the rugged terrain, I started to feel out of my depth. Part of me wished I was still back at the store stocking shelves, but the thought of Teddy pushed me forward. Maybe he had gotten in and the floor had collapsed, or maybe he had knocked his head or something. These reaching thoughts felt silly, but they kept me from thinking of something worse.

Around the right corner, I hugged the wall until I reached the backyard. The place hadn't seen a mower in years; new saplings and bushes had sprouted amongst the fray of tall grass. Old wooden benches had wasted away, and a frayed rope dangled from a tree from the overbearing weight of a tire swing. I looked away from the forgotten yard and focused on the house, stopping in my tracks immediately.

One of the windows had been shattered. Something I would expect Teddy to do if he couldn't find another option. There wasn't much glass on the ground outside, whoever busted it was trying to get in. I looked over the windowsill, my eyes moving from the jagged glass to the nails buried into the wood on the inside sill. There were dozens, each beaten and bent crudely in a hurry. Whoever had put these in, they wanted to keep people out.

I knocked a few pointed shards with my crowbar before climbing in. My gloves were thick and made for such a thing, but I wanted to make sure I didn't get any unnecessary cuts. Last thing I needed was bleeding out on the way back to the car.

My boots met the tiled floor in a crunch of glass. I was in a little bathroom; a small toilet next to a tiny sink, and a glass shower stall tucked next to a water softener. What drew my attention, however, was the immediate tangle in the floor past the glass. It was nearly impossible to tell what it was exactly, but the sight made my heart race. After long seconds of trying to make sense of it, I relented and dug my flashlight out of my pack. The press of the flashlight's button was loud, and the illumination was reeling after being in the dark for so long. Even as I identified the strange mess, I couldn't help but feel confused.

It was a sprawl of extension cords, horribly knotted and strewn everywhere. A multicolored collection of yellow and orange, like someone had made a complete mess of it and dumped it off in the bathroom. Except the pile didn't stop. It continued into the hall behind it, like tentacles feeling out the space. I stood there for a while, the flashlight trailing the lead to try and find the reasoning behind it, but it led out of the room.

For the moment, I tried to ignore it.

Find Teddy. That's why we're here, that's all that matters.

A brief scan of the bathroom told me there was nothing of interest, extension cords aside. The toilet hadn't been cleaned in ages, a black calcified buildup lining the bowl. The water softener was old but wasn't idling. The only thing I could hear was the sounds of my own breathing, and the glass grating beneath my feet. There didn't seem to be any power running in the house.

With the flashlight pointing ahead and the crowbar hefted in my other hand, I moved on from the bathroom, taking a slow step over the ridiculous knot of cords. When I took my first step into the hall, I planted my foot in the only bare spot on the floor that wasn't covered. As I took another step, I nearly tripped. The extension cords were everywhere, a never ending weave that trailed the entire length of the hall, and the sitting room beyond it. Not just a few spools connected together—but *hundreds*, all twisted and looped in a continuous spread that covered the floor as far as I could see.

Three-pronged cords plugged into two. The ones that weren't braided tight to make sure they wouldn't come loose were spliced together and mummified with electrical tape. The more I followed the trail to try and make sense of it, the worse it looked. It had to be *miles* worth of cord.

I took my time navigating the littered floor, stepping slowly as I took in the house around me. The wallpaper was peeling from the walls, and the portraits that hadn't been knocked off the walls had shattered frames, the pictures beneath scratched out angrily. I looked within the sprawl on the floor for clues, any sign that Teddy had been through here. The house was very old, but the mesh of cords kept me from seeing any sign of footprints. The rubber coating squeezed and twisted as I worked my way through what I learned to be the ground floor of a bilevel house that contained nothing but dust covered laundry units on one side, and mold-ridden couches on the other. The stairwell door leading to the upper level was hanging open, held in place by the cords clutter. There was a door next to it, with a bare space in the floor that would accommodate it opening. My first guess would be a basement or a storm shelter.

I decided to clear the upstairs first.

Taking the stairs was a feat in itself. The continuing tangle of cords proceeded both up and down the steps, and I had to ascend sideways to keep from falling. They draped over the steps like a head of hair, dirty strands weaving through each other in the maddening mess. I placed each step delicately, in fear of falling and getting caught in it.

The upper level was split into three different portions; a living room with a fireplace on the side, a dining room with a long table and chairs, and a kitchen. In the middle of it all was the front door, and when I shined the light upon it, I felt my blood run cold. The front door was barred in place, several planks lined across it, each secured with nails driven both into the door itself and the frame around it. The nails were bent and rusted, several of them broken off on their way in. At the foot of the door was a pile of mail; damp and moldy envelopes strewn across the floor of cords.

Different gauges and lengths, all wired into the same maddening mass.

The living room was bare aside from a smoking table, and the ashtray was filled to the brim with cigarette butts. The dining room table was littered with the remnants of picked apart meals, plates and trays splattered with long-dried food that looked like it had been played with. The kitchen was littered with dirty pots and pans, and the dishes that hadn't made it to the fly-buzzing sink were shattered against the counter tops. Even in the rattiest of houses, I had never seen such filth.

I looked around the mass of cords for signs of Teddy, for his flashlight, his gloves, anything—and found nothing but dirt and grime.

The stairs I ascended wound around to the top level; a balconied hallway to a few rooms at each end of the exposed hall. The flashlight served as my eyes as I trailed the corridor from the living room, stopping halfway at the ceiling in the center of the hall, and the dark crevice lurking above.

The attic stairs were pulled down, revealing an open hole in its place. I kept the light on it, feeling a chill that was spreading throughout the room. The cords trailed up there as well, a single braid that looked like it had been drug up it. Transfixed on the attic entrance, my fingers tightened against the crowbar, my breath a cloud of fog. There was something about the attic entrance, something that unsettled me more than the house as a whole. I stared at the attic in the eerie silence, feeling the sweat chill on the back of my neck.

Through the silence, I could hear something; a faint echo that stood my nerves on end. A scream, muffled and far away.

Below me.

I thought of the basement door on the level below. I looked away from the attic and headed back downstairs, traversing the tangle as I went. The scream rang again, and I quickened my pace, nearly sliding down the steps to the landing next to the basement door. The doorknob was cold to the touch. When I opened it, I was hit with the stagnant aroma of decay, a sickening smell that washed into the room.

The basement was dark, a single staircase of planks leading down to bare concrete. I descended, each step creaked under my weight like it was ready to give out at any second. The cords were starting to thin, a cluster of single trails that led into the wall of the basement, into what looked like a hole in the wall. The cinder blocks had been broken apart, leading to another dark expanse.

I heard the scream again, a little louder. It was coming from the hole.

I wanted nothing more than to turn and leave, to climb back out through the bathroom and run to my car. Instead, I climbed in.

The air was thick and musty, the damp smell of dirt and clay clogging my nostrils. There was a tunnel carved out behind the hole, a crude passage that slowly descended into the earth. I followed the trails of cords at my feet, the sweat on my forehead chilling as I worked my way forward.

Through the wicked tunnel I could see a faint glow ahead, like a flickering candle in the dark.

There was a distant *humming*, a slow drone that echoed down the man-made tunnel. The crowbar shook in my hand, and the flashlight beam jittered ahead of me. Fighting every urge to run, my feet reluctantly marched forward, each step bringing me closer to the glimmer underground. The passage was narrow, and I felt the walls close in around me. The extension cords continued to trail ahead at my feet, worn threads leading me deeper into the tunnels.

I came to a fork in the passage; one lit path down the center, and two branching off on either side into total darkness. I shined the light down each, mentally weighing the options as the *humming* droned in the distance. Down the left, I jumped at the sight of rats scurrying away. The right was littered with tiny masses of fur, bigger rodents that looked like they had died painfully, the walls coated in dark, dry splatters. Something had torn them to pieces.

As I looked down the lit passage, I heard the scream again, a weak cry of desperation.

Teddy.

I darted down the center passage, keeping my head low to keep from banging it on the crags above. There was a sickening smell in the air, a toxic smell, like car exhaust. The light continued to spill until I could see clearly without the flashlight, the crowbar held close as the passage started to open up around me. I could see something ahead—a set of steel doors illuminated by a flickering light above, next to an old generator that was chugging away. The generator shook with every chug, the belt looking like it would fly off the pulley at any second.

Chained to the generator was Teddy.

Shackles bound his wrists, and several rusted chains fastened him to the generator, forcing him to lie awkwardly in place. He squinted as I approached, cowering away as I stepped into the light. His face was heavily bruised, and he had several strange gashes on his body, like someone was trying to carve him alive.

He lit up when he saw me, his eyes a mixture of dread and disbelief. He looked happy to see me, but *worried.*

He could barely speak, each word came out as an incoherent drool. I got my picks and focused on the shackles, popping the primitive locks with ease one after another. By the time we got the chains free, he was able to form a sentence.

"Did she see you?"

I looked into his eyes, and his usual carefree demeanor was reduced to a look of pure terror. He looked lost. *Broken.*

"Who?"

Behind us, a mechanical scream echoed in the tunnel. Teddy started to hyperventilate, and I helped him to his feet. His legs shook as he stood, but I ushered him away from the generator, handing him the flashlight so he could navigate while I helped him walk. Together we went back into the darkness, the mechanical scream getting louder as we returned to the fork in the road. It was a quick, dry cackle that sounded like jagged nails on a chalkboard.

The sound was coming from the left tunnel, and in the darkness, I could see a shifting silhouette through a flurry of sparks, moving towards us in quick, twitching motions. The sight of it—whatever it was, made Teddy shake.

"We have to move, now!" I urged Teddy, shoving him along.

We made our way back down the tunnel, the scream haunting us every step of the way. There was another cry along with it, a high-pitched howl that bellowed after us as we bounded towards the hole in the wall. I helped Teddy through, and he wheezed as he struggled to vault the broken blocks. By the time I ducked through, I could see the features of the shape that was chasing us.

Wild, thin hair. Sunken, beady eyes. A nightgown barely hanging off wiry limbs. The shriek of the weapon in her hands.

Teddy limped up the stairs and tripped on the extension cords. The flashlight clattered away, its beam making a kaleidoscope through the dozens of layers of cord. Stumbling myself, I helped him up and guided him into the little bathroom, towards the window we had gotten in from. His limbs struggled to obey, and I had to give him a boost to make it up and out.

As Teddy landed awkwardly on the grass outside, I heard the dual screams racing up behind me. I turned just in time to see the shape flying towards me, the mechanical cry vibrating the air as she brought her weapon down. I raised the crowbar defensively and a flurry of sparks splashed through the dingy bathroom.

Through the glow of sparks I saw an old woman, her face decrepit and rotting beneath tight skin. Clutched in her veiny hands was an electric meat carver, a thin cord trailing behind the bottom, directly spliced into another thick cord. She was strong despite her size, and the dated carver sparked off the crowbar, nearly sawing into my chest, a sick, burning smell emanating from the carver's motor.

Teddy climbed to his feet and reached a hand through the window. I looked into the eyes of the hag and pushed her as hard as I could, sending her into the shower stall in a crash of broken glass. She thrashed wildly through the debris, climbing to her feet through the wreckage, her eyes already back on me.

I looked at the tangle at my feet and tossed the crowbar to Teddy. I knelt down and grabbed an armful of the cords, and just as the hag rushed me again, I threw them at her. She swung again as the cords constricted, the mess of rubber and tape and copper enveloping her like a cluster of serpents. I dove out the window to the sound of sizzles and pops, and as Teddy helped me to my feet, it was joined by the sound of electrocution.

The bathroom became a haze of black smoke, and we watched as the hag seized against her now volatile restraints. As she fell to the floor, her gown caught fire, and the last thing I could see was the simultaneous ignition of melting electrical tape.

Teddy and I fled the house, working our way through the uneven yard as quickly as we could. He rambled apologies about what he had gotten us into, but I ignored him and focused on the road ahead, as well as the house behind us. Even after we were down the driveway, I expected the hag to catch up, screaming while wielding that meat carver. But each time I looked back, there was nothing but the swaying trees that surrounded the house. Trees that looked eager to consume.

By the time we made it back to the agricultural road, we could smell the smoke. The horrid melting smell of an electrical fire and rotting wood wafted through the trees. By the time I helped Teddy into the passenger seat, I could see the glow in the distance.

I started the car and pulled away, the tires spitting gravel as we got the hell out of there.

Heading toward the nearest hospital, we drove through the smoke wafting over the road, our eyes drifting toward the glow within the trees.

The Extension Cord House was lit up like a burning star, a roaring blaze of green and blue hues that reached spitefully towards the sky.

Leaving the madness behind, I glanced in the rearview mirror and felt my stomach twist up. In the dancing shadows of the fire, I swore I could see something shambling out of the driveway, a thin figure with a burning trail behind them, like a leash.

FINGERS FOR TEETH

At first glance, the carnival looked like a derelict camp for squatters. I looked at the flier again, taking in the colorful print and bold, inviting letters. Surely it had to be some kind of mistake.□

SILENT SCREAMING!
PARANORMAL CIRQUE AND CURIO MARKET
Come one, come all! +18 only

The flier depicted images of women holding their own severed heads, malformed birds and cats in jars, and one very disturbing looking clown holding a bicycle horn. It looked like a rip-off from *Tales From the Crypt,* if they were to take their show on the road. When I lowered the crinkled ad and looked at the desolate fairground ahead of me, it looked nothing like the vibrant spooky experience it boasted to be.

It was like a crack den had spilled into a 4-H community center and refused to leave.

"Mom, this looks like shit," I said, cursing with as much emphasis as I could. I didn't want to leave the house in the first place, let alone walk around a camp that reeked of cigarette smoke, burnt hair, and unwashed genitals. You could feel the sleaze of it in the air, a hot musk that whispered into the November night.

"Violet, can you at least *pretend* you want to spend time with me? I saw this ad in the paper and thought it looked like fun. Better than staying cooped up in the house all day," my mom said, her tired face beaming with excitement. It was cold out, and her cheeks were already taking on a rosy shade.

"I have plenty of fun at *home,* thank you," I said, intentionally pushing her buttons. My initial hope was that she'd get tired of trying, and we'd just get back in the car and leave. She would typically fold if I complained and jeered enough, but her usually drained demeanor was replaced by an unusually bubbly mood. I couldn't understand her enthusiasm. Just looking at the place made me feel at risk of HPV.

"At *home,* you just sit in your room all weekend and *ignore me* with your headphones on. Now, c'mon. It's my weekend, and I wanted to do something memorable before..." she trailed off, her hands instinctively falling to her stomach, a habit that had been ingrained in her over the past six months.

"Before your *new baby?*" I said, backing it with as much sting as I could muster. I expected a retort, but her initial reply was a heavy, defeated sigh. She looked wounded, but appeared to get over it quickly.

"Could we just not today, Violet? *Please.* I've missed you so much," she said, pleading. The wind carried on again, and she shivered.

And whose fault is that?

"Yeah. Fine," I said, crumbling up the paper and tossing it. It tumbled away into the darkness of the overgrown lot.

"Thank you," she said, and headed toward the entrance, letting me follow behind.

At the end of the parking lot was a row of tents and stands, each positioned parallel to each other. A string of lights dangled from above, and what looked like handmade lanterns emitted a dying glow over it all. In the pitch black of the night, the vagrant camp seemed to exist purely out of spite. The closer we got, the smaller and shadier it looked. The only definite feature in the congestion was the single walkway that led through the unpacked caravan.

Good. At least it will be short. I thought as we approached the ticket booth.

A large bald man with a mustache stood blocking the entrance of the attractions, smoking a cigarette. He was wearing a Hawaiian shirt, one that seemed to barely contain his broad chest and bulky arms. As we approached, he made a lazy attempt at standing at the ready, taking a final drag from his cigarette before tossing it to the wind. He looked at my mom briefly, before settling his eyes on me. His brow started to furrow immediately.

Mom started with her flirty charm immediately, and I groaned.

"Well, who might you be? The Ring Leader? Or maybe the *strong man?*" she asked, getting our tickets.

"Court ordered community service. And it's eighteen and up ma'am, sorry," he said, apologetically.

"Oh! She's eighteen! She's just a late bloomer is all," she said, lying through her teeth.

"Mom!" I hissed, embarrassed.

"Eighteen? More like *fifteen.* Nice try," he scoffed.

"No really, she's—" she held up her tickets, but he waved them away.

"Am I dressed up like a clown? C'mon now. Rules are rules. Don't make this awkward," he said, already turning away.

"Please, wait—" she grabbed for him, and he stopped, startled. She spoke in a hushed tone, but I could still hear the gist of it.

—please, I've gone through a nasty divorce, and this is my only time with her, I don't get many chances—

His eyes softened before he spoke up. "Ok, *Ok,* Jesus. Settle down, just... give me the tickets," he sighed, and looked around. There wasn't anyone else walking around the event, and the only car that accompanied ours was a rundown baby-blue Taurus that I guessed belonged to him.

"Thank you *so much*," my mom said, handing him the cutout newspaper tickets. He took them and stepped aside before crumbling them and tossing them into a bin next to the gate. My mom pulled me along, flashing me a smile of desperate relief. I followed, but before we made it through the entrance, the man took her arm and halted her. She looked back in surprise, and he started to lean towards her, closer than she looked comfortable with. Just as I wanted to pull her away, he spoke in a hushed tone.

"Look... just keep *her* close, alright? There's some fuckin' weirdos in there. Some of them give *me* the creeps. This isn't some charity event. I wouldn't be anywhere near here if I didn't have to be."

My mom nodded, visibly shocked. I tried to act cool, but his words gave me the chills. My mom thanked him before ushering me along. We were silent as we left him at the gate, neither one of us wanting to talk about the altercation as a whole. I broke the silence.

"It smells like piss in here, mom,"

"Just give it a chance, okay?" she said, pulling me to the first exhibit. Her hands were clammy, but she put on a smile like she usually did. Always the one to act like nothing was wrong. Even as we huddled under the frayed tarps that served as a shelter.

The first stop was strange, but not entirely frightening. A man in a red robe stood amongst several folding tables, each covered entirely in VHS tapes. He stared at us both from beneath his hood, his eyes held open so wide it looked like he didn't have eyelids. His mouth hung agape at an awkward angle, like he was mimicking having a broken jaw. I knew it was fake, but it was still pretty off-putting.

"*Ooooh.* Creepy," my mom said playfully, before running her thumb over one of the tapes. Each was labeled with a scribble in silver marker that reflected in the dancing light above. They looked to serve as price tags, pretty *steep* prices at that. Twenty dollars.

Fifty. One-hundred to three-hundred. In the back row closest to the robed man, they were scrawled in gold marker and priced in the thousands. The tapes themselves felt... dirty. Nasty porn had to be my guess. No wonder it was eighteen plus.

"What's on the tapes?" I asked, and the robed man's eyes darted toward me. It took him a while to respond with his jaw the way it was, but it produced an audible rasp.

"Buy one and find out."

"We're fine, thanks," my mom laughed awkwardly, pulling me with her. It wasn't until then I noticed the little tube TV set up behind him, where one of the tapes was playing silently through lines of static. A woman, sitting in her car, like she was contemplating getting out. She was parked next to what looked like a roped off wall of sand. The only creepy thing about the footage was the fact it looked like she was being recorded without her knowledge.

"Mom ..."

"Oh, look at this one. *Wow,*" she exclaimed, pointing to the next display.

A hag sat on a stool amongst several shelves of curios, trinkets, and taxidermized animals. They each looked real, but had clearly been doctored in their own unique way. A glass-eyed Eagle perched over a long-molded tray of what had to be beans at some point. A penguin covered in peeling blue paint, an old book stitched oddly to where its head should be.

It got stranger the longer I looked, but I couldn't take my eyes off the bizarre collectibles. Just as I wanted to walk away, something else would make me pause.

There was a vampire's coffin propped in the corner, crude steel and rivets held shut by a crisscross of chain. Next to it was a wooden torso bust that showcased a pair of blood-stained prop wings. They looked *lifelike,* as if they were torn from an angel. A dried, dead bat and equally dead preserved spider hung from the top of the tent, their alarming size almost comically drooping down. Rubber replicas, maybe. Bobbing with them was what looked like a dead fae trapped in a glass bubble, with smaller spheres attached to it like a brittle wind chime. Together they fluttered in the wind like ornaments from a condemned Christmas tree.

"Do you think these are real?" I asked my mom, and she answered me softly, her gaze frozen on what the hag worked on diligently in her lap. It was the corpse of what looked like a once living dog—a shepard maybe—her contorted hands working a needle and thread through the blood-stained pelt, where the top half of its skull was missing. Perhaps a roadkill repurpose?

"Of course not, dear," she mumbled, but I could hear the discomfort in her voice. The way the dog's teeth were bared on the bottom jaw, it looked like it had been crushed by a car. There was a menacing vibe to it, like it wanted to jump up and float over at any second.

"All pieces are genuine, *dear*," the hag mocked, looking up suddenly to give my mom a stink face. Her eyes were gray and milky, like they had stopped seeing eons ago.

"My apologies," my mom said, and we quietly moved along.

"This place is a freakshow. We should go home," I whispered, but she ambled forward curiously, dismissing me with a hand. There was something about the place that felt *fake*. Nobody was really trying to sell anything, they just simply appeared to *be* there. And as weird as the props were, they all seemed like they were trying too hard. Like a low budget haunted house a few of the town crazies put up because they had nothing better to do.

"Oh Violet, look at these!" she exclaimed, and I turned to see someone dressed as a plague doctor leaning heavily on a cane. Behind the doctor was a wooden wall decorated with an assortment of masks and fake heads.

The plague doctor beckoned us over weakly, motioning with his beaked face. My mom drifted over, and I reluctantly followed behind her. There didn't seem to be any rhyme or reason to his wares, each one differing wildly from the next. A stereotypical "skinned girl" mask with raspy hair and old makeup. A rusted visage with a set of closed eyes, nose, and a mouth. The faces of five wolf pelts sewn into a single snout in one horrible collection. The severed head of a green haired fairy, complete with a fake-blood drip from the neck. By the time I got to the snowman head with the *flare* for a nose, I couldn't help but roll my eyes. While my mom was enthralled, I couldn't help but feel it was tacky and edgy.

"See anything you like?" the plague doctor said, leaning in dramatically. The cane looked to be plastic, and the costume seemed like a "clearanced" grab from a Halloween store. But the way he *wheezed,* the chocolate-milk gurgle in his lungs... his budget must've went to the voice disguiser hidden in his cloak. He was frail, sure, but any twink could pull on a cheap costume.

"Mom, this is *cringe,*" I sighed, and looked around. The man in the robe and the hag behind us were just watching in silence.

"Just browsing, thank you," she told the man, elbowing me gently. Despite my protests, she pulled me along, giving me a momentary disappointed glare. The exhibits only got stranger as we went on, and grosser the further we went in. The place made me uncomfortable, and stank with a rank humidity of manure and rot. I kept looking ahead for the exit, ready for it to be over, but there was always one more dingy alcove to see.

A blindfolded man slowly applying paint to canvas in weak strokes. The picture portrayed a golem-like monster made of what appeared to be knives, standing under a bleeding sun. *Fake and staged.*

A thin, giantess of a woman cradled the skeleton of a horse, running an old brush through the remnants of its wiry, silver mane. The cascade of her own dark hair obscured her eyes, and the only notable features aside from her dark clothing and incredibly long limbs was her sunken cheeks and overall lack of a mouth. She had to be at least eight feet tall. Protruding from the horse's skull was a chipped, spiral horn. *Makeup, stilts, and plastic bones.*

"That's pretty cool."

"It doesn't make any sense."

"It doesn't have to."

The next was a table set up similarly to the first one, but instead of video tapes it was a bunch of severed hands. Angry flies buzzed amongst them, and each had a price tag tied around the left thumb. Men's. Women's. *Children's.* A shady figure observed from behind the table with his hands stuffed in his hoodie. With the hood pulled up and the plastic mask on his face, he was your average run-of-the-mill "Darkweb" man.

"Oh *come on,*" I said.

The hooded man scoffed.

"Would it kill you to be a little more respectful?" my mom whispered through clenched teeth.

I could tell her patience was finally waning, and whatever guise she had put on was starting to wither away. I saw we were near the exit. The last exhibit was apparently abandoned, as it was just an endless mess of extension cords. All we had to do was walk out and it would be over.

One awkward car ride home, and we wouldn't have to tolerate each other for the rest of the night.

I could've just walked out and held my tongue. But when I saw her resting her hands on her stomach, *her bundle of joy,* I couldn't help but think of how difficult the past several months had been. I opened my mouth with every intention of hurting her, and the words poured so easily.

I'd give anything to take it back.

"Oh, that's *rich,* coming from you," I muttered, just loud enough for her to hear. The words dropped like an anvil, and the Darkweb guy snorted in amusement. I wanted her to hit me, to show me the monster that she was. But her reaction gave me a different kind of pain, one that would hurt more than any backhand ever could.

She just froze, like I had paused her with a remote. Like the sparkle in her eyes had simply faded away.

"*Excuse me?*" she said, but not in a warning manner. Behind the immediate look of betrayal was the aching restraint of tears.

"You heard me," I said, standing as tall as I could. She looked around like I had mistaken her for someone else. She laughed in disbelief, the charade of a smile flickering before fizzling out completely. In the midst of the deer-in-the-headlights stare, her eyes narrowed.

"What's that supposed to mean?"

"You know what it means," I said, looking at her stomach. She looked down and frowned weakly, covering it up like the sight suddenly made her uncomfortable.

"Violet, I-I don't think this appropriate time to be—"

"To be what?" I cut her off. "Honest?"

She scoffed, and a single tear fought itself free. Her eyes flicked around nervously, but the only people around were the strange clerks at the tables behind us. They watched in curious silence. I was happy with the scene, welcoming it.

"Honest? *Wow,*" she said, wiping the tear. It was like I had slapped her. I don't know why I wanted to hurt her so bad, but it was working. I could see her thinking, trying to find a way to skirt around it. Like she always did.

"Did you think I'd just say nothing while everything falls apart?" I asked aloud.

"I don't know what's gotten into you, but I've had enough of it. This isn't the time," she said, shaking her head in disbelief. But before she could pass the pen of extension cords, I spoke up.

"When *is* the time? After you've had the baby? After you get what you want?" I spat. My hands shook, and I stuffed them in my pockets.

"Get what I *want?* You think I—no. I'm not doing this, okay? I'm not going to be embarrassed—"

"*You* don't want to be embarrassed? How do you think I feel? What do you think I tell people at school? Did you ever think of that? All you care about is yourself."

"What?"

"Walking around, like you do. Like you're proud of it. While Dad and I pick up the pieces," she winced as I mentioned him.

"Violet..." she trailed off, looking towards the exit. There was a little table and chairs—the plastic kind for a kid's bedroom—in the walkway. I hadn't really noticed it before, and it seemed to be distracting her. Like it was cutting us off, keeping us from leaving. I was too fired up to care.

"He told me. Everything," I spoke up.

"I don't believe this. Could we just *go, please?* We can talk about it in the car," she begged.

"I don't *want* to go. I want to talk about it now, since you wanted to bring me here so bad. I want to know why," my vision blurred, and I blinked it away. Through the film she just kept shaking her head, chewing her lip to keep it from trembling, her eyes darting back and forth between mine. She was falling apart.

"I just wanted some time with you, is that too much to ask? This isn't how I wanted this to go. I know this isn't fair to you and you don't understand it, but I wanted to wait until you were older. I'm not going to pit you against each other, you don't deserve that. This has nothing to do with you. Let's just *go home. "* she turned to walk away, hugging herself.

"You're right, I *don't* understand it. There is no home anymore. You made sure of that. I thought we were enough for you," I said, trying to keep it together. My face was hot, my ears burned, and I balled my hands into fists in my pockets. I felt the lump in my throat, the sting in my eyes.

"Is that what you think? After all this time, that's what you think of me?" she spun around, throwing her hands in the air. "I thought I deserved better than that."

"If you wanted to leave so bad, you could've done so before you *cheated.*"

"Is that what he told you?" she asked, her mouth hanging open.

"He told me enough."

She was silent for a moment, a sudden rush of anguish visible on her face. Whatever she was bottling up, she was struggling to keep it down. I could see the glass beginning to crack.

"Violet, I…"

"You what?" I demanded, but she wasn't looking at me anymore. My face felt hot against the breeze, the kindling heat rising as she ignored me again. But my annoyance fizzled away completely when I saw what she was looking at.

There was a man sitting at the table. A clown.

The sight of the makeup sent a primal fear through me, the stark white face with an undertone of red that matched his round, shiny nose. I could feel my mother stiffening next to me, and the air itself felt suddenly thinner. His stare turned my stomach, and for the first time in my life, I felt a deep understanding of the word *predatory*. With one hand hovering in front of his mouth, the other squeezed the ball of a bicycle horn, and the *ha-honk* that followed was sharp and unpleasant.

I jumped. My mother didn't. When he spoke, his voice wasn't cheerful or high-pitched. It sounded like it was groaning out of an exhaust pipe.

"Well? What are you waiting for? Let us in on the *joke,*" he said, from his miniature table. His long legs jutted out from the sides of it, and his oversized shoes met underneath. There was an empty tea set arranged across the table's face, dirty plastic that looked to be decades old. A battered doll sat on either side of him; a pirate on his left, and a nurse on his right. They were my size, and he towered above them.

"We were just leaving," my mother said, and the finality of her voice scared me nearly as much as the sight of him. Even from a distance, his eyes burned like little suns—a fade of yellow to maroon around a pinprick of black. I couldn't look away from them, even as my mother took my hand in hers.

"But you can't go. You just got here," he said in a corrective tone. The hand in front of his face never wavered, never showed his mouth. Like his arm was petrified, forced to hold it up. As still as the tattered dolls beside him, watching with their timeworn eyes.

"Let's go, honey," she said in a hushed tone, her eyes holding his. I felt small, suffocated under the tension polluting the air. There was something unspoken unfolding before me, something I didn't understand. In the pooling dread that bubbled around me, I felt the overwhelming regret of the things I had said to her.

Without having to be told, I turned with my mother, and we made our way to the exit. One hand gripped my hand tightly, the other her purse.

The sound that followed was instantaneous and violent. A tumble of plastic against dirt, and the rapid shuffle of shoes getting closer. Like a dog running the length of its leash.

I felt us stop and heard the frantic pull of the zipper.

"Get the fuck away from us!" my mother shouted, and I looked to see the clown was already an arm's length away, his hand still covering his mouth. The can of mace shook in my mother's hand, less than an inch away from his big round nose. She had positioned herself between us, acting as a shield.

The clown stared with wild eyes, and his chest rumbled with every breath. He said nothing for a moment, letting his cartoon-ish frame stand tall over her. The sound he made with every rise and fall made me think there was a lion lurking underneath his ruffled costume.

"You know, I used to tell a joke. The kids... they loved it," he said, his voice full of gravel, "but I've grown *tired* of it. I don't feel like entertaining anymore. Haven't... for a long time in fact," each syllable hissed with the sensation of nails and barbed wire.

"Fuck you, clown," she spat, her finger poised on the trigger. The can trembled in her hand. It only seemed to arouse him.

"What I really want to know is, what kind of delicacy do you have marinating in there?" he growled, his eyes narrowing. My heart pounded in my chest, and my mother gasped.

"I will empty this entire can in your face, I swear to God—"

"Would you? Would you do that for me? Or are you afraid to? Afraid of what I'll do?" he croaked, his voice getting deeper with every word. Behind the hand, I saw the outline curl of a smile.

My mother said nothing, only kept the can aimed at him. It was so close it almost touched him.

Ha-honk.

The bicycle horn squealed at his side, and this time, we both jumped. His shoulders bounced as he laughed—a devil's cackle, dry and hot on the wind.

"You come see us again, now," he said, but he wasn't looking at my mother any more. He was looking at me.

Without a word, my mother started backing us away. With each hesitant step, she never took her eyes off him, and together they kept their hands frozen where they were. Time moved so slowly, I couldn't even feel myself move. As we inched towards the exit, I noticed strange things as we progressed the exhibits in reverse.

The Darkweb man had scooted a set of hands over, leaving just enough room for another pair. The blindfolded man moved his brush against a new canvas, painting what looked like something stretched on a table. The plague doctor hung a new hook on his wall without anything to put up. The hag had finished up work on the dog and placed it amongst the other animals, and had busied herself wiping the clouds from an empty glass jar. The man in the robe had maneuvered his tapes as well, making just enough room for one more.

All of them watched us go, all without a word.

I didn't realize we were outside until I felt the wind chill the sweat on my body. My last look in the tent was burned into my mind, the clown's lanky frame still where we had left him. He hadn't moved the entire time, but I still felt his eyes burning into my skin. His voice ringing in my ears.

You come see us again, now.

We said nothing as we ran to the car. My mother seemed to look for the man outside for a moment, but he was nowhere to be found. The only car left in the lot was ours, like he had just packed up and left. With just the two of us in the cold dark, it was like he was never even there.

I couldn't relax. Even as the engine roared to life, and the headlights lit up the empty gravel drive. I heard nothing but the sounds of my mother's words, soft and reassuring, and could only focus on one thing at a time. She didn't put the mace away but held it in her lap as the other hand white-knuckled the wheel.

"It's okay baby, it's okay," I heard her repeat the words, and it was then I realized I was sobbing. The world moved in a blur, passing trees and streetlights melting at a speed that didn't seem fast enough. It wasn't until we broke out of city limits and merged onto the highway that I felt the weight lift off my chest.

The conversation that followed comes to me in broken pieces.

"I'm sorry."

"We're okay, honey. We're fine."

"I'm sorry I talked to you like that."

"Everything will be alright."

"I don't want you to leave."

"I never abandoned you. I never did."

The things she said later seem scattered the most, but I remember enough to piece it together—to have an answer. When I try to focus on it, I only get the same recorded response, my memory of her telling her side of the story. She spoke strongly at first, but the more she let out, the more the glass cracked, until her eyes ran softly as she navigated the road. She told me of a marriage I saw through a lens, and an endurance through many affairs. One's that were not hers, but my father's. She told me of signs she ignored long after there wasn't an attempt to cover them up.

I listened to her say she stayed until she was no longer allowed to. As tears started to well, I was made aware of the cracks my lens couldn't see, the conversations held behind closed doors. She spoke shamefully of an encounter at a bar outside of town, after she was no longer welcome, and I was no longer on her side. She cried, and I cried with her. I told her how sorry I was, and she told me how she didn't hold it against me, even when I said the things I did. She smiled through the tears, and the grip on the mace loosened. She told me how she loves me, and that she always will.

It was then I felt comfortable enough to relax and rest my head against the window. As we rode in silence, I watched the slow rhythm of lights reflect as we passed underneath them. My eyes grew heavy, and I settled my gaze on the side mirror. I watched the backseat light up and fade to black over and over on repeat and wondered why my reflection looked strange. And I had the slow realization of seeing the hand covering his mouth.

The sound of the horn followed, and everything went black.

I woke to the sound of a bicycle horn, a *ha-honk ha-honk* that seemed to echo around me. My head felt heavy, like it was full of bricks. The light was blinding, and I blinked against it painfully, watching the world come together in the form of a dirty basement. The white paint on the walls was cracked and covered with mold, and it carried the scent of copper and decay. It wasn't long until I heard the twisting, the muffled groans. When I realized what was in front of me, I shrieked, a frantic wail that produced nothing against the pull of duct tape.

In front of me was a wooden table, and on it was my mother. She squirmed and struggled against technicolor restraints, a constrictive wrap of what I recognized to be balloons. They slithered across the table as she struggled, the same vibrant coil pinning her ankles in place and binding her wrists to her chest. Her cardigan was open, and her blouse was raised, just enough to expose her pale, swollen belly.

Lurking above her was the clown, his hand where it always was.

Behind it, his makeup was a runny mess. His wig was in disarray, lopsided on his head and clumped in several places. His eyes were savagely inflamed and wept profusely. Even unfocused, they looked down at my mother with enchanted disdain, carrying an anger so intense it seemed to be boiling the atmosphere around us.

My heart ached when she looked at me, puffy and wild and *apologetic*. I could see her fear, her sorrow, her lack of hope. She kicked and wailed against her confinement, the tendons in her neck straining like tight ropes. When I tried to stand, I felt the same rubbery braid imprisoning me, the stretch and twist of balloons that flexed and bulged but never broke. I struggled until I couldn't, my muscles burning and exhausting until I was nothing but a heaving, crying mess. I could only look in defeat as the clown leaned down and smelled her face, her neck. His hand never lowered. His eyes drifted to me and stayed there.

My mother shook her head, a muted command to look away or close my eyes. But I couldn't help but stare, my vision shifting between her pleading desperation, and the burning eyes that seemed to relish in our suffering.

The clown looked down at my mother like a deity accepting an offering. With a deep guttural groan, he lowered his hand and placed it on my mother's head, forcing her to look at him. My ears rang as we wailed, staring into the abomination that was his maw. They skittered like a spider's legs, dozens of fingers that chittered excitedly. Cracked nails tasted the air and clammy knuckles popped, each of them widened like a living bear trap. The clown's chest rumbled, and the cry that escaped him was deafening and bestial. His jaw cracked with the sound of breaking bones, and his eyes rolled back horizontally as he clamped down.

In one ferocious bite, the clown ripped into her throat, skin parting in an explosion of sugary curls that the fingers raked in greedily. Her skin turned a porcelain pale, and her flesh twisted into a spreading canvas, stitches and yarn replacing eyebrows and hair in an instant. The clown ate and until the color disappeared, the fingers drooling and grabbing at the strands until there was nothing but a hole and torn stitches left behind.

I could see the carnage in glimpses, like a single slide in a film reel. A crack in the reality that shows the gush of blood and gore that she's reduced to, and something much worse than the fingers that reside within the ruffled jumpsuit.

As I grieve the loss, my eyes drift away from the clown and I start to feel sick. I feel my consciousness fading as I look at the canvas skin, to the one detail that remains the same between both worlds. Where the living tissue remains, untouched by the scourge. Alive and writhing.

As the world faded to black, I watched the clown's many fingers walk the surface of the corpse, coming to a stop above the moving globe in a writhing, drooling mess. I close my eyes and feel vomit against the duct tape, as the tearing begins, much louder than the previous.

In the dark, an announcement haunts me. A gravelly voice that echoed in between chews.

"It's a boy."

AUTHOR'S NOTE

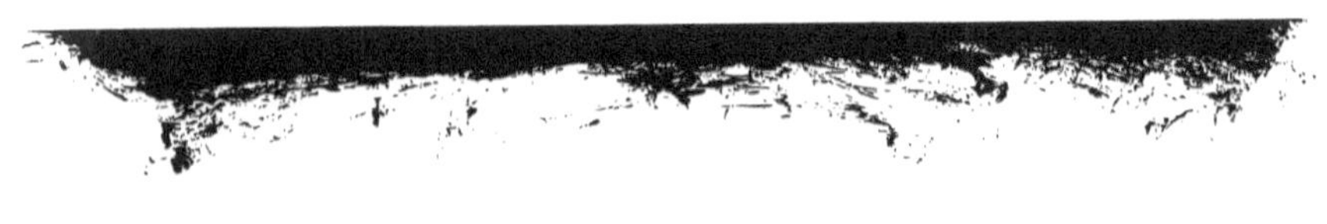

In 2022, my son drew a picture for me. A wonderful scribble of blue and green colored pencil of a totally normal clown, just in time for Halloween. His name was "Cotton", and his favorite thing to eat in the world was cotton candy.

A very normal clown, drawn by a very talented seven year old.

At the time I primarily wrote *creepypastas,* quick and spooky horror that I posted on the internet for kicks—a hobby that would eventually evolve into writing commission work for podcasts that narrated scary stories on a weekly basis. These stories would eventually see paper for the first time in 2023, in little anthologies I self-published if the online readers wanted to support further. And now, published through *Velox Books,* these stories have turned into something way beyond what I initially thought possible—a substantial collection, with characters reappearing years after they were a one-off for fun.

Be it a clown with an appetite for cotton candy, a deer stand, or a powerline, this is a culmination of those works. All these things that used to silently scream in my head on my commute to work, put to paper and immortalized beyond an internet post.

I hope you enjoy them as much as I enjoyed bringing them to life. And I hope when my son finally reads what became of that clown, he doesn't regret the illustration.

I'd like to thank my wife and son for pushing me to challenge myself and write such things, and devote the time to learn what can make a story readable, as well as scary. Many of these ideas came from a child's illustration, a familiar driveway, or a fun day at the beach. If it wasn't for them, I would've given up a long time ago, and these stories would not exist.

Secondly, I'd like to thank my friends and family for their undying support, and putting up with the ramblings that accompany each story as they're created.

Next, I would like to thank all of the wonderful people I have met on my journey writing online, people across the world that burn the same midnight oil that I do. You know who you are, and I appreciate your support from all around the world, at all hours of the day. You guys are the real ones.

I would also like to extend a special thank you to *Velox Books*, for putting on this book and turning it into something extraordinary. They make a damn good book, and there are sequels in here that wouldn't have happened without the opportunity. Cheers guys.

Lastly, I'd like to thank *you, the reader,* for picking up this book in the first place. I hope you found a few of these tales enjoyable, and I hope to entertain you again in the future. *And,* if there was one you liked exceptionally, I'd love to hear about it in a review. I'll see you in the next one.□

Sincerely,□
Jesse Pullins

MORE CHILLS FROM VELOX BOOKS

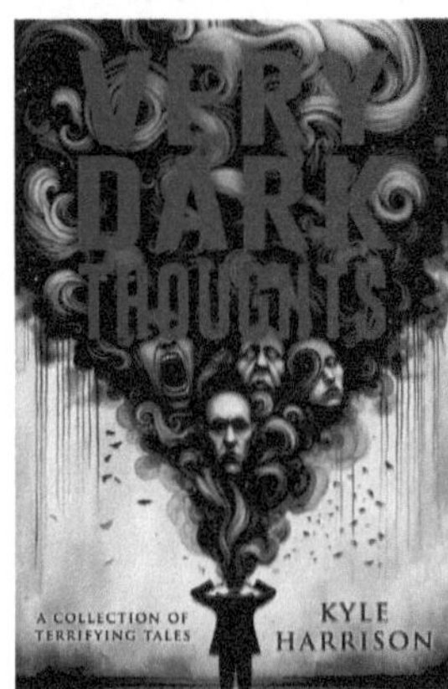

MORE CHILLS FROM VELOX BOOKS

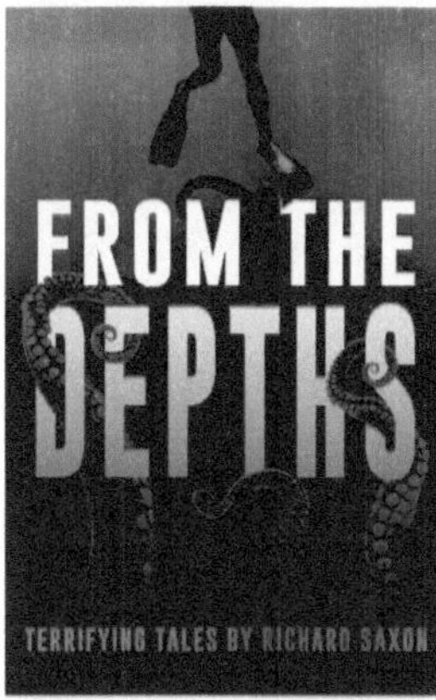

MORE CHILLS FROM VELOX BOOKS

www.ingramcontent.com/pod-product-compliance
Lightning Source LLC
Chambersburg PA
CBHW031046310726
48969CB00007B/2143